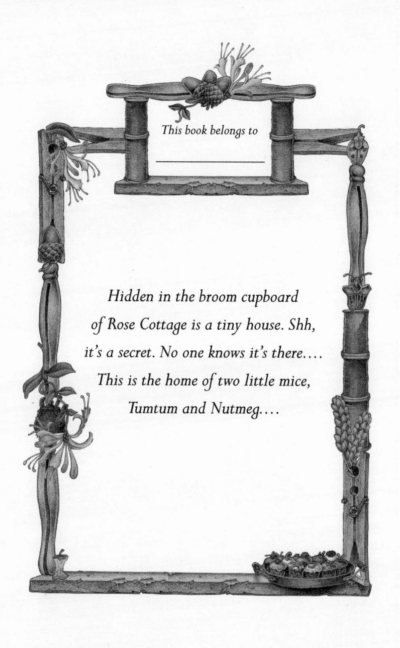

This book belongs to

_____

Hidden in the broom cupboard
of Rose Cottage is a tiny house. Shh,
it's a secret. No one knows it's there....
This is the home of two little mice,
Tumtum and Nutmeg....

# Tumtum & Nutmeg
## The Rose Cottage Tales

Stories by Emily Bearn

With pictures by Nick Price

LITTLE, BROWN AND COMPANY
NEW YORK    BOSTON

Little, Brown and Company

Hachette Book Group
237 Park Avenue, New York, NY 10017
Visit our website at www.lb-kids.com

Little, Brown and Company is a division of Hachette Book Group, Inc.
The Little, Brown name and logo are trademarks of Hachette Book Group, Inc.

First U.S. Edition: October 2010
*A Christmas Adventure* first published in 2009; *A Seaside Surprise*
first published in 2010; and *A Circus Adventure* first published in 2010
in Great Britain by Egmont UK Limited

ISBN 978-0-316-08599-1

10 9 8 7 6 5 4 3 2 1

RRD-IN

Printed in the United States of America

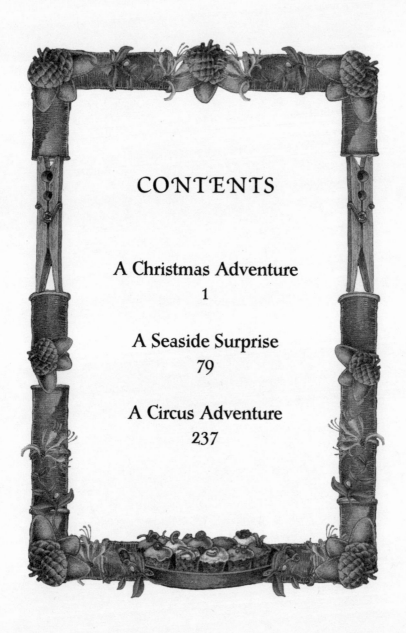

# CONTENTS

# A Christmas Adventure

# Chapter One

Christmas was coming, and Nutmouse Hall looked very splendid.

Tumtum and Nutmeg had put up a tree in the library, with a big pile of presents underneath. And the drawing room and the ballroom and the dining room had all been adorned with tinsel.

General and Mrs. Marchmouse were coming for lunch on Christmas Day, and Nutmeg had been baking and bottling and pickling since early October.

When Tumtum peeked in the refrigerator, his tummy started to rumble. There was a glazed ham and a pork pie and a plum pudding . . . and there were mince pies and jellied fruits and sugared ants, and a big white cake with chocolate reindeer on top.

He could hardly wait for Christmas Day to come.

"Only two more nights to go," he said hungrily.

"Yes, and we've still a lot to get through," Nutmeg fussed.

They had just finished supper, and Nutmeg was sitting at the kitchen table, making a long list of things to do.

"Now let's see . . ." she said, nibbling the end of her pencil. "We have the Christmas crackers to stuff, and the pears to poach, and the silver to shine, and we must polish the ballroom floor, and hang the mistletoe. . . . Oh, and gracious me if I'm not forgetting to glaze the marzipan fruits!"

"I'm sure we'll manage," Tumtum said. "Tomorrow's Christmas Eve, so we've still a whole day to get everything ready. And you've been baking for weeks. Just think what a feast it's going to be!"

Tumtum was very excited. But Nutmeg looked worried.

"I hope Arthur and Lucy have a nice Christmas, too," she said. "When I looked under their tree this morning, there were no presents at all. And their refrigerator was almost bare. Would you believe, I don't think Mr. Mildew's even made a plum pudding!"

2

"Well, I'm sure Father Christmas will bring them something nice," Tumtum said.

"I do hope so," Nutmeg replied. "But I bet their Christmas stockings are full of holes." She looked anxiously at her watch. "Let's go up to the attic and I'll see if they need darning," she said. "It's nearly ten o'clock—the children are sure to be asleep by now."

Tumtum agreed, so he took his flashlight, then they let themselves out of Nutmouse Hall and tiptoed through their front gates into the Mildews' kitchen.

Tumtum went first, cautiously twitching his nose. But there was nothing to fear. The lights were out, and everything was very quiet. He turned and beckoned Nutmeg to follow.

They ran through to the hall, then clambered upstairs to the landing.

They could hear footsteps in the study as Mr. Mildew paced around, trying to think of another silly thing to invent.

They crept past his door and started heaving themselves up the steep flight of wooden steps to the attic.

*Puff! Pant! Wheeze!* It was hard work for two little mice.

Finally, they reached the top and crept out onto Arthur and Lucy's bedroom floor.

They could hear the children snoring softly, but everything else was still. The curtains had been left open, and the floor was pale with moonlight.

"Look, there are the stockings!" Nutmeg said, pointing across the toy train track.

The children had dug them out of the toy chest, ready to hang up on Christmas Eve, and now they were lying in a bundle on the floor.

The mice ran over to them and stretched them out flat on the carpet. They were very nice stockings. Each was made of red felt, with a white rim, and a Christmas tree embroidered on the front.

"This one's got a hole in the toe, just as I suspected," Nutmeg tutted. She ran over to the dollhouse and fetched her sewing basket from the cupboard under the stairs.

Then she sat at the foot of the stocking and started to darn.

*Swoosh! Swish! Swipe!*

Nutmeg always darned at lightning speed.

While she was working, Tumtum shone his flashlight around the room to see if there were any toys that needed to be repaired. Then, suddenly, he noticed a big white envelope propped up on the dresser.

He stepped back and craned his neck up to see who it was addressed to. "Look, dear, they've written a letter to Father Christmas!" he exclaimed. "I wonder what they've asked him for."

Nutmeg looked worried. "Do you think it will reach him in time?" she said. "Tomorrow's Christmas Eve. If they don't go out straight after breakfast, they'll miss the last post."

"I think we had better see what it says," Tumtum said. "Then perhaps we could send Father Christmas a separate letter by Royal Mouse Post, telling him what the children want."

"Good idea," Nutmeg agreed — for the Royal Mouse Post was very efficient. Even if the Nutmouses posted their letter tonight, Father Christmas would be sure to receive it in time.

So Nutmeg abandoned her sewing, then she and Tumtum

6

hurriedly climbed to the top of the dresser, scrambling up by a pair of tights hanging from the top drawer.

They carefully pried open the envelope and tugged out the two letters from inside. Then they stood at the bottom of the page, reading them by the light of Tumtum's flashlight. The first one said:

*Dear Father Christmas,*

*If you have one on your sleigh, please may I have a toy car with lights and a horn and an engine that goes Vroom! — like I wanted last year. I'm sorry you couldn't come then, but I hope you can come this Christmas instead.*

*Thank you very much.*

*Love,*

*Arthur Mildew*

"Well, I'm sure Father Christmas will be able to give him a car!" Nutmeg said. "But I wonder why he didn't give him one last time."

But when they read Lucy's letter, everything became clear. It said:

*Dear Father Christmas,*

*I'm very sorry that you couldn't come last year because the chimney was bricked up. We asked Pa to unblock it, so you could get down this time, but he said he couldn't, because if he did the wind would come in and we'd all be very cold. We hope you'll find another way in. And if you do, I'd like a box of magic tricks, please — like I asked for last year.*

*Love,*

*Lucy Mildew*

"Oh, Tumtum! What are we to do?" Nutmeg cried. "If Mr. Mildew's blocked the chimney, then there's no hope of Father Christmas coming! And the children won't get any presents at all!"

Tumtum looked upset, too. He wouldn't enjoy opening his own presents knowing that the children had none.

Christmas would be spoiled for everyone. Unless...

"*We* shall have to find them a toy car and a box of magic tricks," Nutmeg said.

"But how, dear?" Tumtum asked helplessly. "It's Christmas Eve tomorrow—and the nearest toy shop is five miles away! And besides, I don't suppose they would serve mice!"

"I wasn't suggesting we should go to the toy shop!" Nutmeg cried. She'd had another idea. But it was such a bold one it made her paws feel clammy.

"We must go and see Baron Toymouse," she said.

Tumtum turned very pale. "*Baron Toymouse!*" he stammered. "Gracious! Do you think that's wise?"

# Chapter Two

Tumtum and Nutmeg had never met Baron Toymouse. But they had heard lots of terrible things about him. For Baron Toymouse was infamous for being horrible.

His temper was said to be so bad it could make cupboards shake and doors rattle. And when he got really angry, you could see smoke coming from his nostrils! By all accounts he looked very frightening.

One mouse who had spotted him said that he had eyes as black as night. And another mouse said he had silver claws... and another mouse said that he had teeth as sharp as daggers... and one mouse said he was taller than a full-grown rat!

So no wonder Baron Toymouse's name filled every mouse with dread. There must have been a reason why the Baron was so horrible. But no one could understand what it was — for if you met him, you would think he was a very lucky mouse indeed.

He lived in the nursery of a big, rambling house just up the lane from Rose Cottage. The children of the house had grown up long ago, and no human had set foot in the nursery for many years. So Baron Toymouse had the toys all to himself.

And what wonderful toys they were! Think of any toy you like, and the Baron was sure to have it. And since he was just a mouse, the toys didn't seem like toys. To him, they were life-size.

All day long, he roared about the nursery in his tanks and trains and racing cars and whooshed through the air in sleek model planes. At night, the Baron slept in a big toy castle, with knights in armor stationed around the walls. And when he was hungry, he helped himself to delicious things from his toy candy shop.

Well, a mouse doesn't get much luckier than that!

"The Baron's certain to have a toy car and a box of magic tricks to spare," Nutmeg said. "And if we go and see him, and tell him that Arthur and Lucy won't have any presents on Christmas Day, then I'm sure he'll want to help."

"And I'm sure he won't!" Tumtum said. "You know what everyone says — Baron Toymouse is the meanest mouse alive. Remember what happened last year, when the poor postmouse went to the nursery to deliver him a Christmas card? The Baron frightened him half to death with a toy snake — then he charged at him in a toy tractor!"

Nutmeg sighed. It was true, the Baron was famously ill-tempered. And he was said to guard his toys very fiercely.

But if they wanted to find presents for Arthur and Lucy, then Baron Toymouse was their only hope.

"I'm sure we can win him over, dear," she said brightly. "It is Christmas, after all. Perhaps he'll be in a more festive mood."

Tumtum doubted it. But he could see that Nutmeg's mind was made up.

"All right," he said reluctantly. "We'll go and see him first thing in the morning."

"Oh, thank you, dear!" Nutmeg said.

They put the letters back in the envelope and brushed away any telltale hairs. Then, as soon as Nutmeg had finished her

darning, they hurried back to Nutmouse Hall and tumbled into their four-poster bed. Tomorrow was a big day, and they needed rest. But they both slept fitfully that night. Tumtum dreamed that Baron Toymouse had locked him up in a toy pigsty, and Nutmeg dreamed she was being chased around the nursery by tin soldiers.

She sat up with a fright. And when she looked out of the window, she saw that it was already light.

She turned around and gave Tumtum a shake. "Wake up, dear!" she said nervously. "It's time to visit the Baron!"

# Chapter Three

The Nutmouses had a big breakfast to keep their spirits up. Nutmeg made porridge and pancakes and a fruit salad with cherries on top. And they washed it down with hot chocolate.

"Well, we'd better be setting off," Tumtum said, wiping the crumbs from his whiskers. He always felt braver when his tummy was full.

"We might be gone all morning, so I'll make a picnic lunch," Nutmeg said.

She packed a basket with cold meats and a chocolate cake, and two slices of cockroach pie left over from dinner.

"And we'd better take a Christmas present for Baron Toy-mouse," she said. "I know! Let's give him that box of strawberry creams that I made for Christmas Day. He's sure to like those."

Tumtum's face fell. He had been looking forward to the strawberry creams all week. But Nutmeg was right, they must take the Baron a present. And Nutmeg's creams were so delicious — just think how pleased he would be!

"All right," Tumtum said. And he went off to find some tissue paper and a piece of ribbon to wrap them up with.

Finally, everything was ready. Nutmeg tucked the picnic basket under her arm, and they went to fetch their coats from the cloakroom. Then off they went.

The Baron lived in a big house just down the lane from Rose Cottage, but for Tumtum and Nutmeg it was a long journey, and there was no time to dillydally.

They tiptoed swiftly across the Mildews' kitchen floor and wriggled under the back door into the garden.

It was bitterly cold, and the ground was covered with frost.

"Brrrr!" Nutmeg said, rubbing her paws together.

"Come on," Tumtum said. "We'd better get a move on. I wouldn't be surprised if it starts snowing before the day's out."

They pulled their scarves over their ears and hurried down

16

the garden path and out the front gate. Then they made their way down the narrow lane that weaved through the village. They could see a cat prowling, so they kept to the bank, walking under the cover of the hedgerow.

Eventually, the hedge stopped and they came to a pair of huge black gates with a sign on them that read GRIMSBY HALL.

Beyond the gates was a long drive, and at the end of it was a tall, dark house full of turrets. In one of those turrets was the nursery where Baron Toymouse lived.

Nutmeg trembled. Grimsby Hall looked like a horrible place. Tumtum squeezed her paw, then they hurried on up the drive, huddling together to keep warm.

Eventually, they came to the front of the house. It looked cold and deserted. There was a creeper snaking over the front door, and the windows were boarded with gray shutters.

"The humans must have gone away for the winter," Tumtum said. "No wonder Baron Toymouse thinks he owns the place!"

"Let's try around the back. Maybe there's a way in there," Nutmeg said.

They ran along the front of the house, past a bay tree and a

stone lion. Then they went around a corner, and through a vegetable patch, and around another corner — until eventually, on the far side of the house, they came to a pair of old glass doors leading onto an overgrown terrace. The frame of the door was rotting, and one of the glass panes had come away, leaving a big hole at the bottom.

"Come on, dear," Tumtum said — and they crept inside.

They came out in a long, paneled drawing room, full of tapestries and marble busts. It smelled cold and damp, and the furniture was covered in dust sheets.

They knew that the nursery must be at the top of the house, for that is where nurseries always are. So they started looking for the stairs.

"Let's try through there," Tumtum said, pointing to a door on the far side of the room.

They ran over and peeked through it. And what a sight!

In front of them was an enormous hall, as big as a basketball court, and covered in shining marble.

And leading from it was the biggest staircase the Nutmouses had ever seen. Up and up it went, and on and on,

twisting and turning high into the distance. It had no carpet, and the wood was dark and shiny.

"I suppose we'll have to climb up it," Tumtum groaned.

And so they did.

*Puff! Pant! Wheeze!* Up and up they went, step by slippery step. And no sooner did they reach the top of one flight of stairs than another flight began.

Eventually, when they had climbed five flights and crossed four landings, they arrived in a long corridor full of doors.

They explored it one way, then the other. And at last they came to a pale blue door that had been left open a crack.

And at the bottom of the door, in writing so small only a mouse could have read it, there was a sign that read:

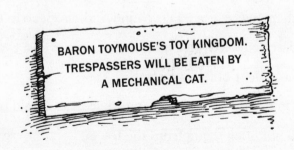

BARON TOYMOUSE'S TOY KINGDOM.
TRESPASSERS WILL BE EATEN BY
A MECHANICAL CAT.

"Oh, dear," Nutmeg said. For it didn't sound at all welcoming.

Then they heard a strange noise coming from inside:

*Clank! Clonk! Clack!*

*Clank! Clonk! Clack!*

They crept around the door and peeked inside. And what an extraordinary sight it was!

They were standing in a vast room, full of the most magnificent toys they had ever seen. It was like a magic kingdom. In front of them was a huge toy farm, with tractors and barns and pigsties, and fields full of cows and sheep.

And beyond the farm was a sprawling model village, with shops and houses and a toy school, and a white palace with beads twinkling from the turrets. And on the far side of the nursery there were a toy fairground and an electric train and an army base crowded with tanks. There was even a toy airport, with a whole fleet of fighter planes.

And in the middle of the room there was a cold black castle, with a gold flag flying from the tower.

Everywhere the room was teeming with dolls and knights

and tin soldiers. They all looked very busy and purposeful—almost real.

But there was no sign of Baron Toymouse.

"Baron Toymouse!" Tumtum called nervously.

No answer.

"Baron Toymouse! I say, are you there?"

Still no answer.

But then they heard the strange *Clank! Clonk! Clack!* again, and this time it was much louder.

The Nutmouses looked around anxiously, wondering where the noise was coming from.

Then all at once a huge voice boomed around the room:

"WHO . . . GOES . . . THERE?"

Tumtum and Nutmeg gulped.

They could not see who was speaking. But they knew it must be Baron Toymouse. They had heard that he always talked through a loudspeaker.

"If you please, Baron, it is Mr. and Mrs. Nutmouse here, from Nutmouse Hall," Tumtum said politely. "If you would be so kind, we have come to ask you a favor."

"*A FAVOR!*" the Baron snorted, as though he didn't like favors one bit. Then: "STAND OVER THERE, BY THE JACK-IN-THE-BOX!" he ordered. "PUT YOUR PICNIC BASKET ON THE FLOOR AND PUT YOUR PAWS ABOVE YOUR EARS!"

The Nutmouses did as they were told.

The next moment they heard a horn blast — then, to their horror, they saw a big backhoe crashing across the floor.

It was bright yellow, and it was coming straight for them. And perched high up in the driver's seat was the most extraordinary-looking mouse they had ever seen.

He was as big as a rat, and he had pink fur, and snarling fangs, and eyes like black pins. He was wearing a long purple cape and a gold crown — and his claws were a dazzling silver.

"Run!" Tumtum cried.

## Chapter Four

Tumtum and Nutmeg flew across the room and hid in the toy police station. The big backhoe crashed after them and came to a stop just in front of the door.

Baron Toymouse stood up behind the wheel and addressed them through his loudspeaker.

"COME AND SALUTE ME!" he shouted.

The Nutmouses crept out, looking very shaken.

They could see now that the Baron's fur wasn't *really* pink — he had dyed it with a felt-tip pen. And his claws weren't *really* silver — they were just painted with glitter.

The Nutmouses thought he looked very silly. But they didn't want him to run them over in his big backhoe, so they did just as he said.

Tumtum gave a salute, and Nutmeg bobbed a curtsey.

Then Tumtum tried to reason with him.

"Now, listen here, Baron Toymouse," he said. "We don't mean you any harm. We've come here because there are two little children living in our cottage, and all they want for Christmas is a toy car and a box of magic tricks.

"But their father's too poor to spend any money on presents, and Father Christmas can't visit them, because their chimney's blocked. So we thought *you* might help."

The Baron glared.

Then he tipped back his head and gave a cold, mocking laugh:

"*ME!* HELP? HA! HA! HA! HA! HA! WHY SHOULD I HELP? WHY SHOULD I CARE? HA! HA! HA! HA! HA! HA!"

The Baron's laugh was so loud it made the whole nursery shake.

The Nutmouses pressed their paws to their ears. They were astonished that any mouse could be so awful.

"Let's give him his present," Nutmeg whispered. "That might put him in a better mood."

26

She ran back to the picnic basket and pulled out the box of strawberry creams.

"WHAT ARE YOU DOING? STOP WHERE YOU ARE!" the Baron boomed.

"We've got a present for you," Nutmeg said, holding it up so he could see.

The Baron's black eyes glinted greedily. He loved presents—as long as they were for him.

"GIVE IT TO ME!" he demanded.

Nutmeg walked back to the big backhoe and handed the box up to him. The Baron snatched it and ripped off the paper.

"CANDY!" he cried gleefully, tearing open the lid.

He opened his mouth and crammed in three at once. But when he tasted the soft strawberry centers, he spat them out with fury.

"STRAWBERRY CREAMS! YUCK! I *HATE* STRAW-BERRY CREAMS!" he cried.

The Nutmouses looked at him in amazement. What a truly horrible mouse he was!

But the Baron hadn't finished yet. He opened his cape and took out a slingshot. Then he loaded it with a cream. And . . .

*THWACK!*

It hit Tumtum smack on the nose. The candy shell burst open, and a big glob of cream slopped down his coat.

"How dare you!" Tumtum shouted.

But then another piece of candy whizzed through the air and smacked Nutmeg on the forehead.

"Ouch!" she cried.

"I'LL TEACH YOU TO COME TRESPASSING IN MY KINGDOM!" the Baron roared, reloading his slingshot.

*PING!*

*THWACK!*

*SPLAT!*

The strawberry creams kept coming.

"Run!" Tumtum cried.

He took Nutmeg by the arm, and they fled across the floor with pieces of candy whizzing past their ears.

They tried to find the nursery door so they could escape

down the corridor. But the room was so big that they couldn't see where they had come in.

They ran on blindly, through the farm and the fairground, then into the toy village, and past the toy school. . . .

All the buildings were locked. There was nowhere to hide.

"YOU CAN'T ESCAPE!" Baron Toymouse boomed behind them.

"This way!" Tumtum shouted, pulling Nutmeg around the back of the church and over a chessboard.

Then at last they saw the door, just a few feet ahead of them.

They ducked their heads and sprinted toward it.

But then they heard a terrifying noise—and when they looked behind them, they each let out a shriek.

They were being chased by an army of mechanical cats!

And sitting astride the biggest cat of all was Baron Toymouse, twirling a lasso made of strawberry licorice.

"HA! HA!" the Baron boomed. "I SHALL TAKE YOU CAPTIVE AND MAKE YOU MY SLAVES!"

The Nutmouses fled for the door.

They could hear the cats clattering after them, faster and faster, and the Baron crying, "HA! HA! HA!" And just as they were about to escape, they heard the lasso swish through the air—and the next moment the loop came down over Tumtum's head, and clutched him around the tummy.

# Chapter Five

Tumtum wriggled and squirmed—but the licorice was pulled tight, pinning his arms to his chest.

"Let him go!" Nutmeg pleaded, trying to tug him free.

The Baron gave a bitter laugh.

"HA! HA! I SHALL LOCK YOU UP IN MY CASTLE AND MAKE YOU SCRUB THE TIN SOLDIERS!" he sneered, clanking toward them on his tin cat.

"Run!" Tumtum shouted, pushing Nutmeg away. "For goodness' sake, run—or he'll catch you, too!"

Nutmeg shot out of the door just before the Baron could grab her. Then she flew along the corridor and started tumbling helter-skelter down the stairs.

Finally she reached the hall and collapsed on the floor. She sat there shaking, listening to her heart going *thump.*

*Oh, what a fool I was to think Baron Toymouse would help us,* she thought wretchedly.

*Tumtum was right, we never should have come. It's all my fault! And if I don't rescue him, Tumtum will spend Christmas Day scrubbing the Baron's soldiers!*

She sat there miserably, wondering what to do. Then suddenly a name came to her like a flash:

*General Marchmouse!*

For if there was any mouse who could rescue Tumtum, then surely it was he. The General was one of the great military heroes of the day. The *Mouse Times* had once described him as "undefeatable"—and that was everyone's view.

*He'll know what to do,* Nutmeg thought. And she decided to summon him at once.

The General and his wife lived in the gun room of the Manor House, which was at the far end of the lane, beyond Rose Cottage. It would take her some time to get there. And when she looked at her watch, she saw that it was nearly noon.

34

If she was to get Tumtum home in time for Christmas, then there was no time to lose.

She got to her feet and raced back across the drawing room, then shot outside through the hole in the glass door. Her legs were trembling and her breath was coming in painful gasps, but she dared not stop. On and on she ran—back down the drive and along the lane and around the duck pond—until eventually she stumbled under the fence surrounding the Manor House garden.

She went the way she and Tumtum always did when they came to visit the Marchmouses—across the croquet lawn, through the apple orchard, then up the clematis on the side of the house and in through the broken windowpane in the cloakroom.

She climbed down onto the cold tiled floor, then crept down the corridor to the gun room.

General and Mrs. Marchmouse lived in the gun cupboard, which was a handsome oak chest, nearly six feet tall. There were no guns in it now because Mr. Stirrup, who owned the Manor House, had given up shooting when his eyesight started to fail.

So the Marchmouses had the cupboard to themselves.

"Thank goodness, they're at home!" Nutmeg said, seeing light spilling through the keyhole.

She raced around to the back of the cupboard, where the General had carved out his front door, and gave an exhausted *Rap! Tap! Tap!*

A moment later, Mrs. Marchmouse appeared. She was holding a pair of scissors and a roll of ribbon. She had spent a quiet morning wrapping her presents for Christmas Day. But when she saw Nutmeg she could tell at once that something was very wrong.

"Whatever has happened?" she asked.

But Nutmeg was too breathless to speak. So Mrs. Marchmouse sat her down in the kitchen with a ginger cookie and a strong cup of tea. Then she fetched the General from his study, where he had been polishing his medals.

And when Nutmeg felt a little calmer, she told them both the whole extraordinary story, from beginning to end.

"So if we don't rescue him, Tumtum will miss Christmas completely," she sobbed. "And he'll spend the rest of his days

locked up in the castle, scrubbing the Baron's toys! And he's never scrubbed anything before and...oh dear...I know he won't like it one bit!"

Mrs. Marchmouse was very shocked.

But the General's eyes were ablaze. *An adventure!* he thought, feeling his blood stir.

Adventures were his first love, and he had been sitting in his gun cupboard all winter long, wishing one would occur.

He had never met Baron Toymouse before—but he had heard all about his magnificent nursery, and he had always longed to go there.

And now here was his chance!

"Do you think you could help?" Nutmeg asked tearfully.

"Help? Of course I can!" the General cried. "I shall summon my brother officers, and we shall take the nursery by force! And, oh, how that mean old Baron will tremble when he sees us coming! We'll seize his big backhoe and tie up his mechanical cats. We'll storm the fire station and pelt the castle with toy grenades! Just you wait, Mrs. Nutmouse! He'll regret the day he ever threw strawberry creams at *you!*"

38

# Chapter Six

To show that he meant business, the General slammed his fist on the table and made the teacups shake.

Nutmeg looked very reassured.

"I shall go and fetch my officers!" the General cried, pulling on his camouflage jacket.

He knew exactly where to find them, for they were all lunching with Captain Snip, who lived just down the corridor in the Manor House drawing room. The General had been invited, too. He had been about to leave when Nutmeg arrived.

He let himself out of the gun cupboard and set off for the drawing room at a run.

Captain Snip lived inside a big wicker sewing basket. It

had been given to Mrs. Stirrup years ago as a birthday present, but she didn't like sewing, so she had tucked the basket away behind the sofa, and now the Captain lived there undisturbed. He had a grand bed made from spools of thread, and his dining room table was a big blue button.

The General hurtled toward the basket and leaped inside.

The other officers were already assembled. There were eleven of them in total, all sitting on pincushions, sipping thimbles of cocoa.

They were dressed in their Royal Mouse Army uniforms, which were bright red and green. And since it was a celebratory lunch, they had all oiled their whiskers. Everyone looked very neat and handsome.

Captain Snip, who was tall and thin with speckled hair, was just passing the peanuts to Colonel Acorn when the General suddenly burst in.

"TO ARMS! TO ARMS!" he cried excitedly. "Mr. Nutmouse has been seized by Baron Toymouse and locked up in his toy castle! And if we don't rescue him, he shall spend Christmas Day scrubbing the Baron's tin soldiers!"

40

Every officer leaped to his feet. Mr. Nutmouse, seized by Baron Toymouse! It was a terrible thought.

"We shall storm the nursery!" shouted Colonel Acorn, gulping his cocoa.

"Hear! Hear!" everyone cried.

They all ran around the sewing basket, arming themselves the best they could with pins and needles, and brass buttons to use as shields.

They set off as soon as they were ready, marching—"Left! Right! Left!"—down the corridor.

Nutmeg and Mrs. Marchmouse heard them from the gun cupboard. "We're coming, too!" they cried. Then they pulled on their coats and hurried to catch up with the officers.

The General led the way. He marched everyone very fast, and it seemed like no time until they reached the gates of Grimsby Hall.

They hurried down the drive, then Nutmeg guided them to the back of the house and showed them the way in through the glass door.

The officers all groaned when they saw the enormous

staircase they had to climb, but after much puffing and panting they finally reached the top floor.

"That's it," Nutmeg whispered, pointing along the corridor to the nursery door.

The officers crept up to it and read the Baron's sign:

BARON TOYMOUSE'S TOY KINGDOM.
TRESPASSERS WILL BE EATEN BY
A MECHANICAL CAT.

"Pah! We'll show him what to do with his mechanical cats!" the General snorted. "Come on, fellows—let's go in and ambush him!"

"Hear! Hear!" everyone cried.

Nutmeg and Mrs. Marchmouse waited in the corridor while the officers tiptoed around the door.

And when they saw inside the nursery, they all gasped. They had never seen such beautiful toys—and everything was mouse-sized.

What a splendid life Baron Toymouse must lead!

The General pointed across the room to the black castle. "Look! That must be where Mr. Nutmouse is locked up," he whispered.

They all studied it through their field glasses. There were toy soldiers firing from the arrow slits, and the entrance was barred with a black gate.

"How will we get in?" the Brigadier said.

Everyone thought for a moment. Then Colonel Acorn pointed to the toy fire station. "I have an idea. Let's seize those fire engines and smash through the gate," he said.

"Good idea," the General agreed. And they all started tiptoeing toward the station.

But then all of a sudden, just as they were cutting through a dolls' tea party, they heard an engine roaring overhead. And when they looked up, they saw a crimson fighter plane swooping toward them. And leaning out of the cockpit was an enormous pink mouse with black eyes and silver claws and a horrible snarl on his face.

# Chapter Seven

The Baron swooped his plane over the dolls' tea party, flying so low he made the teapot shake.

"BOMBS AWAY!" he cried, hurling down a sherbet candy.

"Duck!" the General shouted.

But the next moment the candy smashed against a milk jug—and a thick cloud of powder filled the air.

The officers yelped. There was sugar everywhere, blinding their eyes. And they could hear the roar of the Baron's plane as he looped back toward them.

"Run!" the General shouted.

They stumbled over the cups and saucers, coughing and spluttering. Finally, they saw a white palace looming before them through the haze of sweet powder. It had a flower fairy at the gate and there were pink beads twinkling on the turrets.

"Quick! Let's hide in there!" the General shouted.

The officers staggered toward it and tumbled through the arch. But when they entered the courtyard, they all jumped — for staring down at them was a huge winged dragon, as big as a cat.

"Run!" cried the Colonel, for it looked very fierce.

"Oh, don't be silly," the General said, thwacking the dragon with his pin. "Look! It's only made of tin!"

Everyone laughed, for of course it was very silly to be frightened by a dragon made of tin.

But suddenly they heard a strange noise.

*Clank! Clonk! Clack!*

"What's that?" everyone said.

They rushed to the window. And when they looked out they saw a chilling sight.

The Baron had wound up his army of mechanical cats — and sent them all clattering toward the palace.

*CLANK! CLONK! CLACK!*

46

*CLANK! CLONK! CLACK!*

*CLANK! CLONK! CLACK!*

The palace was surrounded on every side.

"Lock the gates!" the General shouted.

The Colonel and the Brigadier flew across the courtyard and drew the bolts. Then they heard the Baron booming through his loudspeaker, "GIVE YOURSELVES UP AND COME OUT WITH YOUR PAWS ABOVE YOUR EARS!"

When they looked back through the window, they could see him standing on the ramparts of his castle, beside a toy cannon.

He looked huge and pink, and his claws were sparkling.

"We're not frightened of your silly cats!" the General shouted back at him. "Now listen here, Baron Toymouse. You're going to set Mr. Nutmouse free and find us a toy car and a box of magic tricks to give to Arthur and Lucy. And if you don't, we'll make you sorry!"

But Baron Toymouse didn't care. He loaded a marble into his cannon, and fired it across the room.

*KABOOM!*

It smashed straight into the side of the palace and made all

48

the walls shake. The officers cowered under their brass buttons. There were bits of plaster tumbling from the roof.

Finally, the trembling stopped. The General jumped to his feet. "Come on, let's go and teach him a lesson!" he said furiously, brushing the dust off his jacket.

"Hang on," the Brigadier said. "We can't go out on foot — not with all those cats hopping around the palace."

The other officers agreed. It would be much too dangerous. Then Colonel Acorn had an idea.

"I know! Let's ride on the dragon!" he said. He ran across the courtyard and pointed to its tummy. "Look! It's got a switch here to turn it on. It must run on batteries. I'll bet it goes at quite a gallop."

Everyone gathered around to see. They hadn't noticed the switch before.

It was certainly a very fine-looking dragon — there would be room for all of them on its back. It even had a tin saddle.

"Hah! Those mechanical cats will clatter out of the way fast enough when they see *this* coming!" the General said excitedly. "Come on, Colonel. Let's see how she goes."

The Colonel and the Brigadier crawled under the dragon's tummy and wrenched the control to ON.

The dragon shook one leg, then another. It had not been exercised for a long time, and at first it felt rather stiff.

"Quick! Jump aboard!" the General cried, and they all scrambled into the saddle.

The dragon raised its head and gave a long growl. "Grrrrrrr!"

It didn't feel stiff anymore. It reared up on its hind legs and thrashed its tail. Then it tore out of the palace gates and smashed aside a mechanical cat.

"CHARGE!" the General cried, swishing his pin in the air.

# Chapter Eight

The Baron heard a crash. And when he looked down from the ramparts, he saw the dragon thundering across the nursery floor.

"Help!" he cried, hurriedly loading another marble into his cannon. But there was no time to fire — for the next moment the dragon crashed through the castle gate.

The Baron crouched down and hid behind a toy troll.

"Come out, Baron! The game is up!" the General shouted. But the Baron kept very still. The officers stomped around the courtyard trying to find him.

"Where are you?" the General barked.

Then a frightened voice piped up from the corner:

"Over here! I'm over here!"

They all spun around. But it wasn't the Baron they saw. It was Tumtum! And what a sorry sight he was. He was tied to a post and had been left with a bowl of soapy water and a pile of tin soldiers to scrub. You could see he had been having a miserable time.

"Oh, I am so glad you came!" he cried as the Colonel cut him free. "Oh, dear, oh, dear! Do you know, when I'd finished scrubbing the soldiers, the Baron was going to make me clean his toy pigs!"

Everyone agreed that the Baron was very wicked.

"How did you get here?" Tumtum asked anxiously. "Did Nutmeg fetch you? Is she here?"

Before anyone had time to explain, the Brigadier pointed across the castle courtyard and let out a cry. And when the others looked around, they saw Baron Toymouse creeping out of the gate.

"Catch him!" the General shouted.

They raced after him. But by the time they got out of the castle, the Baron had disappeared.

"Where in the world can he be?" the General raged, peering around the nursery through his field glasses.

Then suddenly Nutmeg and Mrs. Marchmouse came running over. They had been watching from the nursery door and had seen what had happened.

"He went that way," Nutmeg cried, pointing to the toy village. "We saw him running past the church!"

"Come on! After him!" the General shouted.

Everyone tore across the room.

"There he goes!" the Brigadier barked, seeing the Baron fleeing down the village street.

"I'll catch him!" Colonel Acorn cried. He leaped into a police car and raced after him with the siren screeching.

The Baron lumbered past the school and the toy candy shop, then dived into the little wooden forest. He had given Colonel Acorn the slip—but the next moment, the General spotted him clambering across a game of solitaire.

"He's over there!" the General shouted.

Then—"This way!" the Captain cried, seeing him duck behind the toy pigsty.

The Baron ran and ran, clutching his crown to his head as he searched desperately for somewhere to hide.

Eventually, he came to the toy fairground and threw himself over the gate. He saw the puppet show tent up ahead and dived inside it, pulling the velvet curtains shut tight. Then he crouched there very still, listening to his heart pounding.

He heard the police car stop and the door slam. Then suddenly there were lots of voices, shouting all around him.

"He's here somewhere!"

"Look in the Ferris wheel!"

"Search the bumper cars!"

The Baron held his breath. "Surely they won't find me here!" He trembled. But the next moment the curtain was ripped open — and he saw everyone peering in at him. They all looked very angry.

The General stepped forward. He looked angriest of all. "Come out, Baron Toymouse. Your reign is over," he said coldly.

The Baron knew when he was defeated. He stepped out of the tent, drooping his ears. He had lost his loudspeaker when

he was running through the forest. And even though he was much bigger than the other mice, he suddenly felt very small.

"How dare you pelt Mrs. Nutmouse with strawberry creams, and chain Mr. Nutmouse to a post, and try to ruin Christmas?" the General thundered. "You should be ashamed of yourself! Colonel, remove his crown."

Colonel Acorn stepped forward, reached up, and scooped the crown off Baron Toymouse's head.

The Baron had behaved very badly—and he fully deserved to have his crown taken away. Still, he looked so wretched, it was hard not to feel a little sorry for him.

"Now look here, Baron—you've still got a chance to make things better," Tumtum said. "All you need to do is find us a nice car for Arthur, with lights and a horn and a big shiny engine. And a box of magic tricks for Lucy. Then we won't be angry with you anymore."

"That's right," the General said. "Or at least—we won't be as angry as we are now."

The Baron considered this for a moment. He didn't want to help—but he could see he was heavily outnumbered.

56

"See that big brown sack over there?" he said sulkily, pointing across the room to the fireplace. "Father Christmas left it here last year—and if you look inside you might find just what you need."

"Father Christmas? Whatever was he doing here?" everyone asked. For there had been no children in the nursery for years.

"He came by accident," the Baron said. "There was a snowstorm on Christmas Eve, and it became so blustery he couldn't drive his sleigh. So he dived down the nearest chimney he could find—which happened to be this one."

Everyone drew in their breath. How exciting to think that Father Christmas had been here!

"Were you awake? Did you see him?" Nutmeg asked eagerly.

"Oh, yes, I saw him all right," the Baron said, showing off. "I was hiding in the castle, and I had a good long stare. And I can tell you he was much bigger than he looks in the picture books!"

"How long did he stay?" Tumtum asked.

"Only an hour or two," the Baron said. "As soon as the storm had passed he went on his way again because he had lots of presents to deliver. But he left that sack behind, with two presents still inside. I heard him mutter something about how he'd tried to deliver them to some children down the lane — but he couldn't get into their cottage because the chimney was blocked. That's why he dumped them here."

Nutmeg clapped her paws in delight. "They must be the presents Father Christmas got for Arthur and Lucy last year!" she cried. "Come on, everyone, let's see what they are!"

The Baron had feared the officers might tie him up, or do something horrible. But they were so excited they forgot all about him.

They raced off toward the fireplace, leaving him standing by the puppet show tent. Then they clambered inside the sack.

The presents were still wrapped, and each one had a label tied to it. One said ARTHUR and the other said LUCY.

The mice tore off the paper. Tumtum and Nutmeg used their teeth and claws, while the officers slashed at the wrapping with their pins. And when they saw what was inside they all let

out a cheer. For it was just what the children had asked for — a toy car and a box of magic tricks, the ones that Father Christmas had tried to deliver last year!

And how splendid they looked. The toy car was a brilliant red, with padded leather seats, and a wooden dashboard with all sorts of mysterious knobs and buttons. And it had a big silver horn, and headlights that gleamed bright yellow.

And the box of magic tricks was full of curious things. There were coins with two heads, and a revolting-looking plastic thumb, and pots of magic potions. And there was a big book of spells called *What to Do to Annoying Brothers*.

"Oh, Tumtum, how wonderful!" Nutmeg cried. "Arthur and Lucy will get their presents after all!"

# Chapter Nine

The officers all thumped each other on the back, delighted that the adventure had turned out so well. But Nutmeg suddenly looked anxious.

"However will we get the presents back to Rose Cottage?" she asked Tumtum. "The car's much too big for us to carry."

"Oh, we won't carry it!" Tumtum replied. "We'll load up the magic tricks, then we can drive all the way home!"

Tumtum beamed. He loved driving toy cars, and it had been a long time since he had last done so.

The Colonel and the Brigadier helped to push the car out of the sack. Then they found a long piece of licorice in the toy candy shop and used it to tie the box of magic tricks to the roof rack.

"I'll take her for a practice run!" Tumtum said, jumping

into the driver's seat. He gave the horn a loud toot. Then—
*vroom!*—off he went, racing around the floor.

"Wait for me!" shouted the General—and he quickly
climbed into a fire engine and started chasing after him. Then
the other officers scrambled aboard the toy train, and the big
backhoe, and the tractors and tanks—and soon every one of
them was tearing around the nursery floor.

*Vroom! Vroom!*

*Toot! Toot!*

"Merry Christmas!" they cried.

What a lovely time they were having, to be sure!

Nutmeg and Mrs. Marchmouse stood by the fireplace,
laughing at them for being so silly. "Really, you wouldn't think
they were officers," Mrs. Marchmouse said. "They're just like a
class of schoolmice!"

Nutmeg nodded. Tumtum was usually such a calm mouse.
She had never seen him as excited as this.

"I wonder where the Baron's gone," she said suddenly.
Everyone was having such a nice time they had forgotten all
about him. She looked back toward the fairground, wondering

if he was still there. And to her astonishment, she saw him standing at the gate, sobbing.

"*Sob! Sob! Sob!*"

His huge shoulders were shaking, and he was crying so hard his tears had made a puddle on the floor.

Nutmeg hurried over to comfort him.

"Don't be so sad, Baron. It's thanks to you that we've found Arthur's and Lucy's presents. Just think how happy they'll be," she said.

But the Baron cried even more.

"Why don't you come and play with the others?" Nutmeg suggested, thinking it might cheer him up a little.

"But I can't play!" the Baron wept. "I don't know how to!"

Nutmeg was very surprised. "But you have more toys than any other mouse in the whole world. You must know how to play," she said.

"Well, I don't!" the Baron replied miserably. "I've never played. And I've never laughed — at least, not a real laugh, not like that." And he pointed toward all the officers, who were giggling and whooping as they played with his toys.

"But why ever not?" Nutmeg asked.

"Because I was never taught to!" the Baron sobbed.

"But you don't have to be taught how to laugh and play!" Nutmeg said. "It's just . . . well, it's just something mice do."

"Well, it's not something that I've ever done!" the Baron said crossly. "And you wouldn't have done it either — not if you'd been born in a wastepaper basket, like I was, and if you'd had to run away from home after you'd seen your mother and your father and your five brothers *and* your seven sisters all whisked away by a cat! You wouldn't have found much to laugh and play about then!"

Nutmeg was very shocked. No wonder the Baron was so ill-tempered.

"How awful for you," she said.

"Yes, it was!" The Baron sniffed. "But I'm a survivor! And I tell you this, Mrs. Nutmouse. Survivors don't laugh and play. Survivors *fight!*"

Nutmeg looked thoughtful.

"Would you *like* to learn how to play?" she asked eventually.

Another big tear rolled down the Baron's nose. "Of course I would!" he sobbed. "I'd give every toy in my kingdom if only someone would teach me. But it's too late. I've been a grouch all my life. Nobody wants to play with *me*!"

"Oh, but how wrong you are!" Nutmeg cried. "Every schoolmouse in the village has heard about Baron Toymouse and his wonderful collection of toys. They'd give their first whiskers to be invited to come and play with you!"

The Baron looked surprised.

"Would they really?" he asked.

"Of course they would!" Nutmeg said. "Just think what fun they'd have! You could teach them how to fly a plane, and drive a tank. And they'd teach you how to laugh and play soon enough! I have an idea. You could invite all the schoolmice here tomorrow, for tea on Christmas Day. What a fine time you'd all have!"

The Baron gave his nose a loud blow. He looked very thoughtful. "Do you think they'd come?" he asked anxiously.

"Come? Of course they would!" Nutmeg replied. "The officers can go around to all the mouse holes tonight, leaving an invitation in every schoolmouse's stocking. How excited they'll be when they find them in the morning!"

"And I could give them all toy swords to play with, and candies for lunch!" the Baron said eagerly.

In his mind's eye, he began to see the young mice swooping and whooping in his fighter planes, and crashing through the dolls' tea party in his toy tanks. And suddenly it all seemed so funny that Baron Toymouse started to laugh.

But this was a very different sort of laugh than the one he used to make through his loudspeaker.

Instead of a "HA! HA! HA!" it was a "Ho! Ho! Ho!" And once he started laughing, he couldn't stop. On and on he went, until his stomach started to ache.

"Why, Baron!" Nutmeg exclaimed. "You don't need the schoolmice to teach you how to laugh. Just look — you're doing it all by yourself!"

# Chapter Ten

The other mice heard the noise and gathered around the fairground gate, watching Baron Toymouse in astonishment.

"Is he all right?" Tumtum asked nervously.

"Oh, quite all right," Nutmeg replied. She handed the Baron her handkerchief, for he had started to splutter.

Finally, the Baron stopped laughing. Then he wiped his eyes and addressed everyone very solemnly.

"These toys are for sharing," he said, sweeping his arm around the room. "And from now on I will run this nursery as a park, where every mouse in the village can come and play. It will be the finest mouse playground in the whole world. And it will open tomorrow, on Christmas Day!"

Everyone cheered and slapped the Baron on his enormous back.

"I'll bring my son!" said the Brigadier.

"And I will bring my niece!" said the Colonel.

"And I'll bring myself!" said the General, who was longing to take a ride in the Baron's plane.

The Baron looked very pleased.

"Now, hurry, hurry!" he cried. "You must go at once, or Arthur and Lucy won't get their presents in time for Christmas! And remember, you have to deliver an invitation to every schoolmouse in the village, asking them here tomorrow!"

"We will," the officers promised.

They were anxious to get going, for they had a lot of mouse holes to visit. And they didn't want to be home late for Christmas Day.

They all shouted goodbye to the Baron. Then they tucked their pins under their arms, and off they marched—"Left! Right! Left! Right!"—out of the nursery door.

The General and Mrs. Marchmouse stayed behind, for Tumtum had offered them a ride home in Arthur's car.

"Jump in," Tumtum said.

So they all climbed inside, the General and his wife in the back, and Nutmeg in the front. Then Tumtum wriggled in behind the steering wheel, and — *Vroom!*

Off they sped, through the door, and along the corridor, and *Bounce! Bounce! Bounce!* down the stairs.

"Goodbye!" Baron Toymouse shouted.

"Goodbye! Goodbye! Merry Christmas!" the officers cried, as the car clattered past them.

"Merry Christmas!" Nutmeg cried back, waving her handkerchief from the car window.

Tumtum drove with great skill. They raced around the sofa legs in the drawing room, then he pressed his paw down hard on the accelerator, and they shot out through the hole in the glass door.

Then off they went, over the vegetable patch, up the drive, and *r-r-r-r-r-r-r-r-r, rrrr-roar!* down the lane.

The night was icy cold. Nutmeg shivered and pulled her scarf around her face. The car window was still open, and she could feel something damp on her nose. And when she looked into the beam of the headlights, she could see a flurrying cloud of white.

"Oh, everyone — look! It's started snowing!" she cried. "It's going to be a white Christmas!"

"We'd better get home quick — we don't want the car getting stuck," Tumtum said. He hunched over the wheel and drove faster and faster as the snow pattered against the windshield.

Tumtum dropped the General and Mrs. Marchmouse at the gates of the Manor House.

"Good night, and see you tomorrow," the General said. "We shall come on our toboggan!"

"Good night!" Nutmeg cried.

Then Tumtum looped back down the lane and sped toward Rose Cottage.

They drove through the front gate, then raced up the garden path until they reached the back door.

The door was falling apart, just like everything else in Rose Cottage. There was a gap at the bottom where the wood had rotted away — just wide enough for the car to drive through.

Nutmeg clung to her seat while Tumtum skidded across the kitchen floor, then shot into the drawing room.

"There they are!" she cried, seeing Arthur's and Lucy's stockings hanging beside the fire. The children had even left Father Christmas a plate of cookies on the hearth—so they must have been hoping he'd come!

Tumtum and Nutmeg jumped out of the car, then they grabbed the bottoms of the stockings and tugged them to the floor.

Finally, Tumtum drove the car into one stocking, and they pushed the box of magic tricks into the other.

"Just think how pleased the children will be when they find them in the morning," Nutmeg said. "They'll think Father Christmas managed to get in after all!"

"Since we've done Father Christmas's job for him, do you think we could eat his cookies?" Tumtum asked longingly.

"Oh, I'm sure he wouldn't mind," Nutmeg said. She hadn't eaten since breakfast, and she could feel her stomach rumbling, too.

They climbed onto the plate, then sat down on either side of one of the cookies and started breaking off little chunks.

It had been a very long day, and they both ate hungrily. Tumtum sighed contentedly. It was wonderful to feel full and fat again.

"Well, I'm glad that adventure's over," Nutmeg said eventually. "Just think, dear. You might have spent Christmas Day cleaning tin soldiers!"

"I wouldn't have liked that," Tumtum yawned. He had eaten rather a lot, and he was feeling very sleepy.

"I suppose we'd better get back to Nutmouse Hall," he said. But they were so tired it was tempting to stay a little longer.

And by the time the clock chimed midnight, they were both fast asleep on the plate—dreaming of plum puddings, and tin dragons, and mechanical cats that went "Boo!" in the night.

On Christmas Day, Arthur woke up first.

And when he looked out of the window he gave a shout:

"Lucy, look! It's snowed!"

Lucy jumped out of bed and ran to look out. The snow had come thick and fast, and the whole garden was glistening white.

"Do you think Father Christmas managed to get in?" Arthur asked anxiously.

"Come on, let's go and see," Lucy said.

They pulled on their robes and ran downstairs.

Nutmeg, who had been curled up against a cookie, woke with a start.

She sat up and gave Tumtum a shake.

"Quick! Get up, dear!" she said urgently. "The children are coming!"

They leaped off the plate and shot under the bookcase. A moment later the children ran in.

"Look—he *has* come!" Lucy cried when she saw their two stockings bulging on the floor.

Lucy pulled out her box of magic tricks and peered at it in delight. It was full of mysterious-looking things. She took out the little bottles of potions and studied the labels. There was a

pink potion called "Shrinking Liquid: For Making People Smaller," and a bottle of green potion called "Swelling Liquid: For Making People Grow," and a bottle of jet-black potion called "Vanishing Liquid: For Making Annoying People Disappear."

She couldn't wait to try them all on Arthur.

And Arthur had never seen such a splendid car. It had lights and an engine, just like he had asked for, and when he honked the horn it was so loud it made Lucy jump.

"This is the best car ever!" he said, racing it around the sofa. "Wasn't it clever of Father Christmas to find a way in!"

"I knew he would," Lucy said. Then she noticed the plate of cookies. "He can't have liked them much—he's only eaten half of one!" she said.

But half a cookie was an awful lot for Tumtum and Nutmeg. And had the children turned around just then, they would have seen two rather fat mice waddling out the door.

# A Seaside
# Surprise

# Chapter One

Tumtum was sitting at the kitchen table with his head slumped in his paws. "*The seaside?* But we can't possibly go to the seaside," he groaned. "We might be chased by a crab!"

Tumtum had heard very frightening things about the seaside. He didn't like the sound of it at all.

But Nutmeg's mind was already made up. "If Arthur and Lucy are going to the seaside, then we are going, too," she said firmly.

"When are they leaving?" Tumtum asked miserably.

"Tomorrow morning," Nutmeg replied. "I must say, I wish they'd given us a little more warning!"

She had only learned of the trip a few minutes ago, when she had poked her head into the kitchen and heard the children discussing it.

"They're going to stay with their uncle Jeremy," she went on. "And would you believe it, Mr. Mildew is going to let them travel by train *all on their own*! We'll have to stow away in one of their backpacks and keep an eye on them."

Tumtum scowled. The last time he'd stowed away in a backpack it had been very uncomfortable. "How long are they going for?" he asked.

"A week," Nutmeg replied.

"*A week!*" Tumtum cried. A week is a long time in a mouse's life. "Who will look after Nutmouse Hall?" he asked.

"I'll ask Mrs. Marchmouse to come and keep an eye on things," Nutmeg said busily. "Now don't look so glum, dear. The sea air will do us good. And a week will go by in a flash. You will love it once you're there!"

"No I won't," Tumtum muttered. The very thought of the seaside made him shudder. He knew he wouldn't like it one bit.

"I hope this doesn't turn into another adventure," he said glumly.

"Of course it won't, dear," Nutmeg replied.

But Tumtum wasn't so sure.

The following day, late in the afternoon, there was a sudden *Toot! Toot!*, then a loud clatter of brakes as the express train drew into Mousewall-on-Sea.

"Hooray! We're here!" Arthur shouted, leaping from his seat. They had been cooped up in the train compartment for hours, and he was longing to get out.

Lucy sat up, looking a little startled. She had been asleep, and her toes were full of pins and needles.

"Can you see him?" Arthur asked, pulling down their bags from the luggage rack.

Lucy pressed her nose to the window and peered into the throng of faces on the platform.

"There he is!" she cried.

She had only met Uncle Jeremy once before, and that had been ages ago, before she turned seven. But she spotted him at once, for he looked quite different from anyone else. He was round and comfortable, with a red nose, and a waistcoat stretched so tightly over his stomach that the buttons looked as if they were about to go *Ping!*

"Here's your bag," Arthur said, heaving down Lucy's back-pack. "Wow! What did you pack in it? It weighs a ton!"

"Well, at least I didn't bring four pairs of shoes like you did," Lucy replied.

But Arthur was right—when she pulled her backpack onto her back, it did feel very heavy. It was odd, for she was sure she hadn't packed much.

But as soon as they got off the train she forgot all about it, because there was so much else to think about.

The children had never been to Mousewall before, and it all felt very strange. Uncle Jeremy drove them home through a maze of little wriggling lanes, with hedges so high you couldn't see over them.

Then finally they came to the top of a very tall hill—and when they looked down, they could see the sea, spread out like a big sheet of silver.

Uncle Jeremy stopped the car for a moment so they could admire the view.

In front of them was a thin road, twisting down to a

crescent-shaped bay circled by green cliffs. In the middle of the bay there was a little beach, and a cluster of cottages.

"That would be a nice place to live," Arthur said enviously.

"Well, I'm glad you think so," Uncle Jeremy replied.

"Is that where *you* live?" the children cried. "Oh, how wonderful!"

Uncle Jeremy looked very pleased. Then he started the car again and drove all the way down the hill until they came to a white cottage with fishing nets piled in front of it and a sign above the door that read:

The children piled out of the car and looked around in delight. The cottage was on a narrow lane, and just on the other side of the lane was a tall stone wall, with steps leading down to the beach. They had known that Uncle Jeremy's house was by the sea—but they hadn't expected it to be as close as this.

And Smugglers' Keep was such a mysterious name for a

cottage, they felt something exciting was sure to happen to them there.

"Come in and I'll show you your room," Uncle Jeremy said, hauling their bags out of the car. He opened the front door, and the children ran inside to explore.

Smugglers' Keep was very old. The furniture was dark and dusty, and the floorboards creaked. The children's bedroom was at the top of the house, and it had tall wooden beds and a pointed window looking out to sea.

"Well, you sort yourselves out, then we can have dinner," Uncle Jeremy said, dropping their bags on the floor. "Mrs. Blythe's made a fish pie."

Uncle Jeremy had already told the children about Mrs. Blythe. She was his housekeeper, and she did everything for him — or at least everything that Uncle Jeremy felt he couldn't do himself, such as cooking and cleaning, and making beds.

"We'll be down in a minute," Arthur said. He hadn't eaten anything since lunch, and his stomach was rumbling.

"I'll take this bed," he said, claiming the one closest to the window.

"All right," Lucy said, thinking it wasn't worth arguing about. She tossed her backpack onto the other bed, the one closest to the door — and as it landed, she heard something squeak. "Goodness, doesn't this room feel funny," she said. "Everything creaks!"

Arthur ran to open the window, and that creaked, too.

Then — "Wow!" Lucy said. "Look at that!" For tucked beside the wardrobe was a big dollhouse, with pale pink walls and peppermint shutters. Lucy thought it was the prettiest dollhouse she had ever seen. And yet when she peeked inside, it was quite empty. There was not a stick of furniture, not even a bed. "I wonder whose it is," she said. "It's odd that it doesn't have anything in it."

"Oh, I don't know. Maybe it belonged to Uncle Jeremy when he was a little boy," Arthur said. He wasn't interested in dollhouses. He wanted to explore the beach.

But Lucy thought it was rather mysterious. "If only we were here longer, I could make some furniture for it," she said. She was still gazing at it as she pulled open the strings of her backpack and started tugging the contents out onto the bed.

"Oh, come on," Arthur said impatiently. "We can unpack later. Let's eat first."

"Hang on. It won't take long," Lucy said.

"But I'm starving!" Arthur groaned, hovering at the doorway.

"Oh, all right," Lucy sighed. Then she dropped the backpack back on her bed and ran after him down the stairs. And it was just as well she didn't finish unpacking, or she would have found something most unexpected hidden in her clothes.

# Chapter Two

Tumtum and Nutmeg clambered out of Lucy's backpack and onto the bed, pulling their luggage behind them.

And what a lot of luggage there was!

Four suitcases, two deck chairs, a folding table, a beach umbrella, their swimsuits, Tumtum's fishing net, Nutmeg's sewing basket, and two picnic baskets—one for savories and one for sweets.

No wonder Lucy's backpack felt heavy!

The Nutmouses were very stiff. They had been traveling all day long, squashed up inside one of Lucy's slippers.

"I'm aching all over," Tumtum groaned.

Nutmeg was aching, too. But once they had stretched their legs on the bed they began to feel better.

"Come on, we'd better find somewhere to hide before the children come back from dinner," Nutmeg said.

They stood gazing around the room, searching for a suitable hideaway.

"What about that dollhouse?" Nutmeg exclaimed. "Doesn't it look grand? It would make a splendid home for us!" The windows had been left open, and she could see inside the rooms: "We wouldn't be getting in anyone's way — it looks quite abandoned," she said. "It's not even furnished!"

Tumtum shook his head. "It would be much too obvious — Lucy's sure to look inside it, and imagine what a fright she'll get if she finds that we've moved in. Let's try under there," he suggested, pointing to a big dresser in the corner. It was raised on four legs, so there would be just enough room for them to stand up underneath it.

"We'll be well hidden — the children will never see us," he said.

Nutmeg agreed, and that was how the adventure began.

They dropped all their luggage over the edge of the bed,

94

then they climbed down the blankets and dragged everything under the dresser.

But it was not at all agreeable. It was dark and gloomy, and the floor was covered in cobwebs.

"Surely we could find a nicer hiding place than this," Nutmeg said, scrunching her nose. "Why don't we try inside one of the bedside tables?"

Tumtum shook his head. "If we camp in a bedside table, the children will be sure to find us," he said. "This is much safer. And once we've set up our picnic table it will look more homey."

He dug out the lantern so they could see what they were doing. But when he shone it around, they both stared in surprise. For in the wall behind them there was a little round mouse hole, with a green door and a shiny brass bell. And above the door was a sign that read:

LORD SEAMOUSE OF SEAVIEW HOLLOW

LORD SEAMOUSE OF
SEAVIEW HOLLOW.

"Gracious!" they exclaimed. They hadn't expected to find another mouse living here.

"Perhaps we'd better go and hide somewhere else," Nutmeg said anxiously—for Lord Seamouse sounded like a rather frightening name.

"Don't be silly, dear," Tumtum replied. "Now that we're here, we must ring the bell."

"Oh, please don't!" Nutmeg cried. But before they could decide whether to ring it or not to ring it, the door opened and a fat white mouse in a green waistcoat appeared. This was Lord Seamouse and, goodness, he did look lordly! He was wearing a watch on a gold chain, and a pair of satin slippers.

Lord Seamouse hadn't seen another mouse for weeks, so he was rather startled. "Are you here to collect the rent?" he asked anxiously.

"No, no, nothing like that," Tumtum reassured him. "We're here to look after Arthur and Lucy."

Lord Seamouse looked very baffled—for, of course, he had never heard of Arthur and Lucy. So once the Nutmouses had introduced themselves, they had to tell him the whole story—about how they were the children's secret guardians, and how they had traveled all the way from Rose Cottage in the bottom of Lucy's backpack.

Lord Seamouse nodded and looked very impressed.

"So we hope you won't mind if we camp under your dresser for a few days," Nutmeg said finally.

"You'll do no such thing!" Lord Seamouse said in a booming voice. "You will both stay in Seaview Hollow with me! Now come on in. You're just in time for dinner!"

Tumtum and Nutmeg looked delighted.

Lord Seamouse helped them drag everything inside. He was astonished by how much luggage they had. But when he saw Tumtum's family crest on the suitcases, he supposed they must be rather grand.

When the last case had been dragged in, Lord Seamouse gave them a tour of his mouse hole. It wasn't at all like the sort of mouse hole you would expect a lord to live in. The rooms were small and poky, and the furniture was all mismatched. The beds were made out of matchboxes, and the dining room table was a yogurt cup.

When he had shown them around, Lord Seamouse laid a tray with tea and ginger cake, and scones with clotted cream and jam on top. Then they all sat down beside the drawing-room fire, in armchairs made out of seashells.

"Have you always lived here?" Nutmeg began.

"In this hollow? Oh, gracious no!" Lord Seamouse spluttered. "In fact, it's a rather long story—"

And he was about to tell it, but then all of a sudden the doorbell rang.

Lord Seamouse jumped.

"Two sets of visitors in one afternoon!" he said in astonishment. This really was unusual. He hurried through to the hall, wondering who it could be.

The Nutmouses waited by the fire. Presently they heard footsteps in the hall, and a voice that sounded oddly familiar. And when Lord Seamouse showed the new arrival into the drawing room, they could hardly believe their eyes!

"Well, dear me!" Tumtum stammered. "If it isn't General Marchmouse!"

## Chapter Three

The Nutmouses were astonished. They had seen the General yesterday, and told him about their trip. But he hadn't mentioned anything about coming too.

"How did you get here?" Tumtum asked.

"In the same backpack as you!" the General replied shiftily. "I was hiding in one of Lucy's shoes. I crept onboard last night. I've never been to the seaside, so when I heard you were going, I decided to come too!"

"Does Mrs. Marchmouse know you're here?" Nutmeg asked. Poor Mrs. Marchmouse. The General was always running away from home, and it made her terribly nervous.

"She'll know by now," the General said, looking a little guilty. "I left her a note on the breakfast table."

Tumtum and Nutmeg sighed. They should have known better than to tell the General about their trip — for he could never resist an adventure. And whenever he turned up, trouble seemed to follow. Which is why the Nutmouses were not altogether pleased to see him.

But Lord Seamouse didn't know how troublesome the General could be. He was delighted to have another visitor. "I'll go and make some more tea," he said. "And I believe I've got some jam tarts left, unless that nuisance of a cockroach has eaten them all."

Lord Seamouse hurried off to the kitchen. But as he reappeared, there was a huge crash that made the whole mouse hole tremor. The paintings shook on the walls, and the cups rattled in their saucers.

"Help!" Lord Seamouse cried, ducking behind the tray.

"There's no need to worry. It's only the children coming back," Nutmeg said calmly.

The children crashed and banged all the time in Rose Cottage, so she and Tumtum were quite used to it by now.

But Lord Seamouse looked horrified. There hadn't been

any children at Smugglers' Keep in his lifetime, so he didn't know how noisy they could be.

"They won't give you any trouble," Nutmeg assured him. "And if the weather's fine they'll spend most of their time out-doors."

Lord Seamouse sat down in his seashell, feeling rather shaken.

"What do human children *do*?" he asked curiously.

"Oh, lots of things," Tumtum replied. "They play soccer and hide-and-seek, and they bake cakes and they make model airplanes, and they read books—"

"*They can read?*" Lord Seamouse asked in astonishment.

"Oh, yes," Nutmeg replied. "And they can write, too!"

Lord Seamouse stroked his whiskers. He looked deep in thought.

"Do you think they could read a map?" he asked eventually.

"Of course," Tumtum said. "They are a highly intelligent breed."

"Then they might be just what I need!" Lord Seamouse said excitedly.

"How do you mean?" Nutmeg asked.

Lord Seamouse got up and walked over to his desk. He opened the drawer and took out a brown envelope labeled

Then he pulled a piece of crumpled paper from it and passed it around so everyone could see.

"It's a map!" the General exclaimed. He always loved a good map to read. And this one looked very intriguing.

It showed a beach covered in sand castles, with a line of big craggy rocks down one side. The biggest rock had its name written beside it — Stargazer — and it was marked with a black cross.

"What does it all mean?" he asked excitedly.

"It is a treasure map!" Lord Seamouse said in a hushed tone. He leaned over and traced it with his paw. "The beach is just here, in front of the cottage. And the cross marks where the treasure is hidden — in a cave inside Stargazer!"

"What treasure?" the General asked.

"Why, my treasure, of course!" Lord Seamouse replied. "The Lost Treasures of Seaview Manor!"

"Seaview Manor?" everyone asked, looking very confused.

"Yes, Seaview Manor," Lord Seamouse said impatiently. "You must have noticed it when you were traveling across the bedroom floor. It's the finest manor house in all of Mouse-wall!"

"Oh, you mean the dollhouse!" Nutmeg said. "Yes, we did admire it. But it looked abandoned. Does no one live there?"

Lord Seamouse sighed. He could see that he would have to explain everything from the very beginning.

"The last person to live in Seaview Manor was me!" he said. "And oh, you should have seen the house then! I lived just as a Lord should. There were tapestries and chandeliers and four-poster beds...and a piano and a Ping-Pong table...and the drawing-room chairs were upholstered in chintz! Every room was appointed to the highest standard. And if you could only have seen the dinners I hosted in the dining room! Do you know, my dears—the table could seat twelve!"

Lord Seamouse wiped a tear from his eye. Thinking about his old home always made him sad.

"Whose dollhouse was it?" the General asked.

"It had belonged to Uncle Jeremy when he was a little boy," Lord Seamouse said. "He used to keep it downstairs in the drawing room. But it got in the way—so one day he dumped it up here. And that's when I moved in!"

"Did Uncle Jeremy never see you?" Nutmeg asked.

"Oh, no," Lord Seamouse replied. "Uncle Jeremy seldom comes up here. And besides, he's much too old to be playing with dollhouses now."

"So what happened to all the furniture?" Tumtum wondered. It was clear Lord Seamouse hadn't brought any of it to Seaview Hollow. Everything here was very shabby.

"It was stolen—every last stick!" Lord Seamouse said. "I went out for a stroll one day, and when I came home, Seaview Manor had been stripped bare. They took everything—the wardrobes, the beds, the soup bowls—they even took my stuffed beetles!"

"Who?" everyone cried.

"Beach mice," Lord Seamouse said distastefully. "Bad apples, who sleep rough in sand castles — Mousewall's full of them. Anyway, word had gone around that I had a lot of fancy things, and one day a gang of them came up here and stole everything. My cleaning mouse, old Mrs. Moptail, was polishing the silver when they arrived, and they tied her up! When I got home, she was the only thing left!"

Everyone looked very shocked.

"What a terrible story," Nutmeg said.

"It certainly was," Lord Seamouse replied. "Mrs. Moptail was in a dreadful state. And I couldn't even make her a cup of tea — because the rotters had taken my kettle! Well, I couldn't stay in Seaview Manor without any furniture. It felt much too bleak. So I moved in here, to Seaview Hollow. And of course it's perfectly cozy and all that.... But ... well, it's not quite the same."

The others nodded in sympathy. They could see why the Hollow must seem like quite a letdown after life at the Manor.

"Was Uncle Jeremy upset when everything disappeared?" Nutmeg asked.

"Oh, he never bothers with the dollhouse. He hasn't even noticed that the furniture's gone," Lord Seamouse replied. "But of course the thieves took his teeth, too!"

"*His teeth?!*" everyone cried.

"Yes, his teeth," Lord Seamouse said. "All his milk teeth — you know, the ones that fell out when he was a boy. I found them in Seaview Manor soon after I moved in. They were hidden under a bed!"

"Was there a full set?" Tumtum asked.

"Oh, yes. A full set!" Lord Seamouse replied proudly.

Everyone gasped, for human teeth are very valuable things. If a wicked mouse creeps up in the night and plucks one from under a child's pillow, he can trade it with the tooth fairies for a gold coin. So just think how much a whole set would be worth!

"How did they end up under the bed?" Tumtum asked.

"One of the tooth fairies must have hidden them there when Uncle Jeremy was a little boy," Lord Seamouse replied. "Each time she collected another tooth from under Uncle Jeremy's pillow, she would have added it to the pile, until eventually there was a full set. They were very dusty when I found them. You could tell no one had touched them for years."

"But why would the tooth fairy have left them there so long?" Nutmeg asked.

"Oh, you know what fairies are like," Lord Seamouse said snootily. "Very silly creatures—always forgetting things. The poor fairy probably couldn't remember where she'd hidden them!"

"What did you do with them?" Nutmeg asked.

"I polished them up and displayed them in my drawing-room cabinet," Lord Seamouse replied. "All my visitors admired them—and they became quite a talking point. That was my mistake, of course. Because soon every mouse in the village seemed to know that there was a full set of milk teeth in Seaview Manor—so I suppose it's hardly surprising I was robbed."

"Couldn't you catch the thieves?" Tumtum asked.

"Oh, we tried," Lord Seamouse said. "Every policemouse in Mousewall was on The Case of the Missing Teeth. And our local *Mouse Gazette* ran a big story on it—there was even a reward on the rascals' heads. But they were very clever. They didn't leave a single clue."

110

"So, what about this map?" the General asked impatiently.

"That's the exciting part," Lord Seamouse said. "The other day, the postmouse arrived here with a letter. And to my surprise, it was from one of the thieves himself—a fellow called Black Jaw. And very strange it was, too. He said he was the only one of his gang left. The rest of them came to a sticky end, or so he told me. Apparently they were stealing candy from the village shop, and they got trapped in a tub of sherbet!"

"Ooh! How horrible," Nutmeg said.

"What happened to Black Jaw?" Tumtum asked.

"He got away," Lord Seamouse said. "And without the others to egg him on, he began to mend his ways. He stopped thieving and started cleaning mouse holes for a living. But he didn't get much work because all the mice around these parts knew him as a crook. So he decided to move farther up the coast and start his life all over again.

"But he felt so bad about robbing Seaview Manor that before he went, he sent me this map, showing me where the gang had hidden everything they stole. And he said that the teeth were still there, too."

"How thrilling," the General cried. "Then we must go at once and get everything back!"

"Oh, that would be out of the question," Lord Seamouse said. "Stargazer's the tallest rock on the whole beach—as tall as two grown men! If you stand in front of it, you can see it's full of caves. The treasure is hidden in one of them, but the rock face is much too steep to climb."

"Then how did Black Jaw's gang get there?" Tumtum asked.

"They went up the Secret Tunnel inside the rock," Lord Seamouse replied. "But the tunnel begins in the Grotto. And to reach the Grotto you have to cross the Rock Pool. And if you try to cross the Rock Pool, you'll be gobbled alive by the Crabby Crab! Well, Black Jaw's gang had a big boat, so they could get past him all right. But I've only got a raft, so I'd never survive!"

Nutmeg turned pale. She didn't like the sound of the Crabby Crab one bit. But the General was fearless: "Who cares about your silly crab! I shall find the cave!" he cried.

Lord Seamouse laughed. "I wouldn't try it, old boy—you'll come to a sticky end!"

The General scowled. He didn't like being laughed at.

112

"Well, if you don't let me try, then you'll never get your treasure back," he said grumpily.

"Oh, but I will—now that these two human children have appeared!" Lord Seamouse beamed. "Don't you see? *They* can climb up the rock and dig the treasure out. It would be no trouble for those giants. They could carry the entire contents of Seaview Manor home in a pillowcase!"

Lord Seamouse's face shone. At long last, he might see all his lovely things again.

Nutmeg looked anxious. "Are you sure they wouldn't come to harm?"

"Of course I am," Lord Seamouse replied. "The rock wouldn't seem very big to them. And the Crabby Crab won't give them any trouble—it will flee to the bottom of the pool when it sees two humans coming!"

"I think it's a capital plan," Tumtum said. "Just think how thrilled they'll be!"

Nutmeg agreed—the children would love a treasure hunt. "I'll leave the map on Lucy's bedside table tonight, and I'll write them a letter, explaining exactly what to do," she said.

Lord Seamouse hurried to his desk and found her a piece of paper.

Everyone was very excited. But General Marchmouse had suddenly become quiet. Crabby Crabs! Caves! Secret Tunnels! Why, this was just the sort of adventure he craved. And he didn't see why Arthur and Lucy should have all the fun. He shot a sideways glance at the map, which Lord Seamouse had left on his chair. *Forget the children*, the General thought slyly. *I'll find the cave first! And I'll bring back the teeth! And oh, just think what a hero I will be!*

# Chapter Four

Later that evening, when the children were asleep, Tumtum and Nutmeg crept out to leave the map on Lucy's bedside table.

When they got back to Seaview Hollow, Lord Seamouse made some cocoa. Then they sat up talking in the drawing room. But General Marchmouse didn't say much. He had decided that as soon as the others went to bed, he would sneak out and steal the map back! Then he would set off for the beach at dawn and find the treasure all by himself!

He fidgeted in his armchair, wishing they would all turn in. But on and on they chattered. The General found their talk very dull. His long day had tired him. He became drowsier and drowsier, and his eyelids felt like lead.

By the time Nutmeg offered him another mug of cocoa, he was fast asleep.

She gave him a prod, but he didn't stir.

"We might as well let him sleep here. There's no point moving him," Lord Seamouse said.

Tumtum pulled off the General's shoes, and Nutmeg tucked a warm blanket around him. Then they all went off to bed, leaving the General snoring in his armchair.

When the General woke up in the morning, he felt very foggy. He heard the clock chime seven, and he rubbed his eyes, trying to remember what he was supposed to do.

Then he gave a gulp. "*THE MAP!*" he cried.

He threw off his blanket and sprang from the chair. Then he let himself out of the mouse hole, and crept into the children's room.

But when he peeked out from under the dresser, he let out a howl. He was too late! Arthur and Lucy were already awake.

They had found the map and Nutmeg's letter. And now they were sitting staring at them on Lucy's bed.

The General seethed. If only he hadn't fallen asleep!

Lucy was reading the letter through the magnifying glass attached to Arthur's penknife.

"Oh, hurry! What does it say?" Arthur said impatiently.

Lucy held it up to her face and read it out loud:

*Dear Arthur and Lucy,*

*You will have noticed that there is a big dollhouse in your bedroom — but you would never guess what a mysterious tale it has to tell. For it isn't really a dollhouse. It is the home of a Very Important Creature called Lord Seamouse. But one day, all of Lord Seamouse's beautiful treasures were stolen by a gang of thieves. He was quite heartbroken — and since he no longer had a bed to sleep in, he had to move out.*

*But now, my dears, you might be able to help. Attached to this letter you will find a map of the beach in front of Smugglers' Keep. Be sure to take good care of it, for this*

*map is very special. It is a Treasure Map, showing where all*
*the treasures from the dollhouse are hidden. If you follow*
*the map, you will be able to find them and put everything*
*back in place.*

*Love,*

*Nutmeg*

*P.S. Say nothing of this to Uncle Jeremy. We don't want*
*any grown-ups interfering in our adventure.*

The children were astonished.

"What sort of creature do you think Lord Seamouse is?" Lucy asked.

"I don't know," Arthur said. "And if he's half as secretive as Nutmeg, then we won't be seeing much of him!"

Lucy frowned. It was true. Nutmeg never appeared. But she was longing to know more about this mysterious-sounding Lord Seamouse. "With a name like that, maybe he's a mouse," she said.

"Don't be silly," Arthur said. "Mice don't have titles. Now come on! Let's hurry up and find this treasure!"

They quickly got dressed and had breakfast, and then they set out.

"Stay in front of the house, where I can see you, and don't go climbing any rocks," Mrs. Blythe fussed.

"We won't," they replied, hurtling out the front door.

They crossed the lane and ran down the steps to the beach. It was a very small beach, about the size of a tennis court, and this morning there was no one else there. There were just some rowboats propped against the wall and three canoes lying upside down in the sand.

On one side of the beach there was a little harbor full of fishing boats. And on the other side there was a line of tall black rocks snaking down to the sea.

The children shaded their eyes, for it was already hot, and the sun was making the sand glare.

Arthur pulled out the map, and then they tried to work out what was what. But the drawing was so small that the lines just looked like squiggles.

Lucy had to have a long look through the magnifying glass before she could make any sense of it.

"I've got it!" she said finally. Then she held the map so Arthur could see and pointed each thing out:

"There's the sea . . . and that's the harbor wall . . . and these shapes must be those big rocks over there. And the cross is on the biggest rock. So that must be where the treasure's hidden! Come on! We'll find it in no time!"

"Hang on," Arthur said. "What are these?" He was pointing to some tiny marks on the side of the map, next to where the cross was drawn.

Lucy peered through the magnifying glass again. The marks were so small that at first they just looked like dots and dashes. But when she looked harder, she could see that they were letters.

She studied each one very carefully and read them aloud. "S—T—A—R . . . Stargazer!" she said. "That must be the name of the rock where the treasure's hidden!"

Stargazer. It sounded very mysterious.

"Come on. Let's go and find it!" Arthur said.

They ran over to the rocks and stood looking at them from the sand. In the front, the rocks were smooth and flat, like giant pebbles. But the rocks behind were much bigger. Some were as tall as a front door.

"That must be Stargazer," Arthur said, pointing to the tallest rock of all.

It was very different from the other rocks. It was black and ragged and shaped like a witch's hat. And there was a big rock pool in front of it—but not the kind anyone would want to paddle in. The water was dark and thick with seaweed.

The children could see from where they were standing that Stargazer was full of little nooks and crannies. The treasure could be hidden in any one of them.

They scrambled up onto the boulders and started exploring around the bottom of the rock. They searched and searched, digging their hands into each little groove—but all they found was an old golf ball.

Then Arthur climbed a little way up the rock, hanging on by the juts and grooves, and poked around in the caves higher up. The smallest cave was the size of a jam jar, and the largest was as big as a laundry basket. To a mouse, they would have seemed quite spacious. But they did not take Arthur long to

explore. He groped his hands around each cave in turn—but there was no treasure.

Soon the whole morning was gone.

"Come on," Lucy said eventually. "We'd better get back—it's nearly lunchtime."

"The treasure must be hidden in one of those little caves right at the top," Arthur said, jumping back down.

Lucy frowned. "Then how will we reach it?" she said.

"Look! I can climb up onto that," Arthur said, pointing to a place where the rock bulged to form a small platform. "Then I'll be able to reach across."

"All right," Lucy said. "Let's come back this afternoon and try."

Arthur tucked the map into his pocket, then they ran back to the cottage.

Mrs. Blythe opened the door. She was holding a pair of oven mitts, and her face was red from cooking. "Goodness, look at the state of you!" she exclaimed, seeing Arthur's blackened hands. "You'll need a good wash before lunch. Whatever have you been doing?"

"We were just playing around the rock pool," Lucy said guiltily, remembering that they had promised not to climb on the rocks.

But Mrs. Blythe did not seem very interested.

"Hurry up, dears, lunch is ready," she said, bustling back into the kitchen. The children ran to the bathroom to wash.

"Don't let Uncle Jeremy see the map!" Lucy whispered.

"Of course I won't," Arthur said, patting his pocket. "I'm not that stupid!"

But unbeknownst to him, there was danger lurking.

As the children walked into the dining room, General Marchmouse — dressed in his green summer uniform — was hiding under the sideboard, following their every move.

He watched as Arthur sat down in the chair closest to him, and he saw him reach a hand into his pocket to check that the map was still there.

*Aha!* the General thought.

He waited until Mrs. Blythe had gone back to the kitchen. Then he sprang out from his hiding place and shot up Arthur's leg like a bullet.

Arthur felt something tickling him and darted a hand to his pocket — but the General had already snatched the map in his paws and leaped to the floor.

Uncle Jeremy, who was sitting at the opposite side of the table, was suddenly aware of something flashing across the carpet toward the door.

He put down his fork and frowned. It looked like a mouse. In fact, he could have sworn it was a mouse. But it was *green*!

He assumed his eyes must be playing tricks on him — and he took off his spectacles and gave them a good polish.

The General moved so fast that the children, who were facing the other way, did not see him at all.

But Arthur was rummaging in his pocket. Then he turned to Lucy, looking very pale.

"The map!" he whispered. *"It's gone!"*

# Chapter Five

It was only when lunch was over and they had run back upstairs to their bedroom that Arthur was able to tell Lucy what had happened.

"I felt something tickling my leg, then when I looked in my pocket, the map wasn't there!" he said. "Something took it!"

"But what?" Lucy said. "It must have been something very small."

Arthur shuddered. "It felt like a spider," he said. "It moved very fast, that's for sure. And it obviously knew what it was looking for—it went straight for my pocket, then shot off like a bullet!"

"A spider? But that's impossible," Lucy replied. "Spiders can't read maps!"

Arthur shrugged. "Maybe it was a mouse, then."

Lucy shook her head in bewilderment. "But mice can't read maps either."

The children felt very confused. Someone had taken the map, that was for sure. But whoever could it have been?

"We'd better write Nutmeg a letter, warning her that the map's been stolen," Arthur said. "If there's someone else after the treasure, then she might know who they are."

Lucy agreed, so they found a piece of paper and wrote a hurried note:

*Dear Nutmeg,*

*Arthur was looking after the map while we were having lunch, but then something ran up his leg and dived into his pocket and stole it. He didn't see what it was, but it felt like a mouse. And now they might be looking for the treasure, too. But we'll make sure we find it first.*

*Love,*

*Arthur and Lucy*

They folded the letter in half and propped it against the lamp on Lucy's bedside table, where they had found Nutmeg's letter that morning.

"She'll know what to do," Lucy said, feeling reassured.

"I hope so," Arthur said. "But now let's go back to the beach and start looking again. We've still got a lot of caves to explore."

They ran downstairs. But Uncle Jeremy was waiting for them in the hall. "How would you like to come fishing?" he asked brightly. He was holding some rods and a canvas bag stuffed with tins and reels.

The children flinched. Normally they would have loved to go fishing. But this afternoon they had treasure to find.

"Come on, jump in the car," Uncle Jeremy said, grabbing his straw hat. "We might catch something for dinner."

"We'll have to go with him," Lucy whispered, fearing Uncle Jeremy would be hurt if they refused.

"But what if someone else finds the treasure while we're gone?" Arthur asked.

"They won't," Lucy said firmly. "We'll only be away a few hours. No one's going to find the cave as quickly as all that."

But unbeknownst to the children, General Marchmouse had already set off. And now he was clambering down the steps to the beach, with the map clutched tightly in his paw.

"I shall find the teeth first! And just let anyone try to stop me!" he muttered.

He jumped off the bottom step into the sand and stared around him in astonishment. He had never been on a beach before, and it was a thrilling sight. There were huge strands of seaweed, coiled like snakes, and exotic shells colored pink and blue and green. And there was ridge after ridge of golden sand, stretching as far as the eye could see.

The beach may have seemed small to Arthur and Lucy. But to General Marchmouse it was like a desert.

He took out his map and noted in which direction the rocks must be. And when he looked through his field glasses, he could just see them, black and hazy in the distance.

He tucked the map back into his breast pocket and set off toward them. It was a long way, and the sun was very hot. Soon his throat felt parched, and he could feel the sweat trickling down his shirt.

On and on he tramped, until eventually a dark shadow fell on him. And when he looked up, there they were—a range of huge black mountains, towering out of the sand!

He took out the map again, trying to work out which one was Stargazer.

"It must be that one!" he cried excitedly, gazing up at the biggest mountain of them all. And when he saw how steep and craggy it was, his heart soared. The General loved danger—and he was sure to find it here.

At the base of the rock there was a smooth, flat boulder, about a foot high. He climbed onto it, pulling himself up by a strand of seaweed. When he got to the top, he saw the Rock Pool— and then even the brave General Marchmouse felt a pang of fear.

It stretched before him like a vast lake, and it looked horribly cold and slimy! On the far side of the pool, he could see the opening of a small black cave. He knew it must be the Grotto

that Lord Seamouse had told them about, where the Secret Tunnel began.

But how would he reach it? It was much too far to swim.

*I need a boat!* he thought. And he started searching around the rock for something he could use.

Then suddenly he saw a Popsicle stick lodged under a pebble. *That will make a fine surfboard!* he thought. He tugged it free and lowered it into the pool. Then he slithered down onto it, so that he was lying flat on his tummy, and pushed himself off from the bank.

He waited until the stick had stopped wobbling. Then he dipped his paws into the pool and started to paddle.

The water was icy cold, and he couldn't see below the surface. He didn't like it one bit, but he kept his eyes fixed on the cave and paddled on as fast as he could.

*At least there's no sign of the Crabby Crab*, he thought. *Lord Seamouse was probably making that up!*

But when he was halfway across the pool, he felt a sudden tremor beneath the water, then all at once a huge pink beast reared up in front of him.

The General lay on his Popsicle stick, quivering like jelly. It was the pinkest, most hideous creature he had ever seen. It had claws like nutcrackers, and a huge pink head with monstrous pink eyes goggling straight at him.

*The Crabby Crab!* The General trembled.

The Crabby Crab fixed him with a very crabby stare. Then it reached out a long pink claw and grabbed him around the stomach.

"Put me down!" the General squealed. But the Crabby Crab just squeezed him tighter. The General saw his life flash before him. He thought he was going to be gobbled up in one bite.

The Crabby Crab was drawing him closer and closer, and its crabby mouth was gaping.

*My pistol!* the General thought desperately. But he had left it at home. Then suddenly he remembered his slingshot. With a thumping heart, he fished it from his pocket and loaded it with his last peppermint.

He had catapulted many a beetle before, but never a beast as big as this. He aimed very carefully, for he knew he could not afford to miss.

*TWANG!* went the elastic.

Then *THWACK!* went the peppermint, as it hit the Crabby Crab smack in the eye.

The beast reared backward, giving a roar of pain. He loosened his claw and let the General fall — *plop!* — into the pool.

The General kicked furiously, gasping for air as the seaweed and the black water swirled all around him. Then he felt something clonk against his shoulder — and when he looked up he saw the Popsicle stick floating beside him. He hauled himself onto it and started thrashing furiously back across the pool, not daring to turn around. When he reached the bank, he hauled himself out of the water. Then he raced to the edge of the rock and slid back down the seaweed into the sand.

And then he ran and ran and ran — faster than he had ever run before.

*Puff! Pant! Stumble! Wheeze!*

On and on he fled until Stargazer and the Rock Pool and the Crabby Crab were all far behind him. Then finally he collapsed, panting, in the sand.

Everything was suddenly very quiet. All the General could hear was his heart going thump.

His backpack was soaking wet, and his clothes were covered in slime.

"The map!" he yelped, fearing he had lost it. But when he felt in his pocket, it was still there.

He fished it out carefully, for the paper was soggy, and held it in the breeze to dry.

It was late in the afternoon, and he still had a long walk home to Seaview Hollow. He felt very wretched. He was cold and hungry, and he knew Tumtum would be furious with him when he got back.

He staggered to his feet and started trudging miserably through the sand.

But the beach seemed to go on forever.

*I must be nearly there*, he thought, when he had been walking for a very long time.

But there was still no sign of the steps in the wall. He looked through his field glasses, but all he could see was sand. Never-ending sand.

"Oh, dear," he said. "I'm lost!"

## Chapter Six

Tumtum and Nutmeg and Lord Seamouse had spent a pleasant day sunbathing on the drawing-room windowsill.

It was nearly four o'clock when they finally packed up their picnic basket and made their way back to Seaview Hollow.

"I wonder why the General suddenly darted off like that, before we'd even started our picnic," Nutmeg said as they climbed upstairs.

"Oh, I don't know," Tumtum said sleepily. "He probably went off exploring. You know the General. He can never sit still."

But Nutmeg still felt uneasy. It was unlike the General to miss lunch.

And as they were walking home across the children's bed-room floor, she noticed the letter on Lucy's bedside table.

"Oh, look, Tumtum!" she said eagerly. "Quick, let's see what it says! Perhaps they've found the treasure already!"

Lord Seamouse waited on the floor while Tumtum and Nutmeg climbed up the bedcover and hopped onto the bedside table. They unfolded the letter under the lamp—but when they saw what it said, their faces fell.

For the Nutmouses guessed at once that it was the General who had stolen the map from Arthur's pocket.

"I should have known he's been up to no good!" Tumtum said angrily.

They dragged the letter back down to the floor. And when they told Lord Seamouse what had happened, he looked very alarmed.

"I hope the General's not still out on the beach," he said. "The tide will be coming in soon!"

Nutmeg turned pale. "We must go and look for him!" she cried.

"The beach is huge. We'd never find him," Lord Seamouse said. "And there's no point in us all getting into trouble."

Tumtum was worried, too. But he agreed with Lord Seamouse that it would be foolish to go out looking for the General now.

"Just you wait, dear—he's probably on his way home already," he said, giving Nutmeg's paw a squeeze. "And you know how greedy he is. He's sure to be back in time for dinner!"

Just then they heard a thunder of feet on the stairs. It was Arthur and Lucy, back from their fishing trip.

"Come on, quick!" Tumtum said—and they all darted under the dresser.

Lord Seamouse let them back into Seaview Hollow, then they waited anxiously for the General to reappear.

But by dinnertime there was still no sign of him. Nutmeg had made a seafood pie, yet somehow no one had much appetite.

They sat in an unhappy silence, listening to the tick-tock of the clock, and to the breeze whistling under the mouse hole

140

door. Nutmeg pulled her shawl tighter. The thought of the General all alone on the beach made her shiver. Oh, if only he would come home!

They were quite right to be worried. For General Marchmouse was having a terrible time.

He was stumbling through the sand, with no idea which way he was going.

Goodness, he was tired!

Gradually it got dark, and the moonlight started playing tricks on him. At one point, he thought he could see a strawberry ice cream bar in the distance. He hurried hungrily toward it—but when he got there it was just a pink shell. He trudged on a little farther. Then he saw a sight that made his heart leap. Just ahead of him, parked in the sand, was a beautiful silver car. *Hooray!* he thought. *I can drive home.* But when he reached it, he let out a howl of dismay. It was just a lemonade can!

Eventually, when he thought he couldn't walk another step, he saw a castle up ahead. He staggered toward it. And this

time his eyes weren't deceiving him. It was quite real—and what a splendid castle it was! It had a moat and a drawbridge and tall yellow turrets, all built out of sand.

And there was light spilling from the arrow slits.

*That's good*, he thought. *There must be someone at home!*

Whoever lived here was sure to know the way back to Smugglers' Keep.

He walked across the drawbridge, which was made from a plastic spoon. Then he poked his head through the archway.

There was a campfire burning in the corner, and a delicious smell of roasting flies. There was no chimney, so the room was full of smoke. The General couldn't see much.

"Is there anyone at home?" he called.

No reply.

"I say, it's General Marchmouse here! Is there anyone at home?" he called again, in a more commanding voice.

Then he heard a horrible laugh. Laughs aren't usually horrible, but this one was. It was harsh and cackling, and it cut through the air like a whip.

Then out of the smoke there appeared the nastiest-looking mouse the General had ever seen.

He was tall and gray and whippet-thin, and he was dressed in a black cape and tall scarlet boots. And he had bloodshot eyes and yellow fangs. And — most unusually — purple claws.

He gave the General a long icy stare. And yet when he spoke his voice sounded as smooth as molasses.

"I am Purple Claw," he purred. "*Doooo* come in. You're just in time for dinner."

The General didn't like the look of him one bit. But he was so hungry, the thought of a roasted fly lured him in.

Purple Claw didn't have much furniture. There were just two pebbles to sit on, and a purple shell for a bed.

"Sit down," Purple Claw said, pointing to one of the pebbles.

Then he took the frying pan from the fire and tossed the General two roasted flies, keeping four for himself.

"It's very kind of you to share your dinner with me," the General said nervously.

There were no plates or cutlery, so they ate with their paws.

It was so smoky, the General could barely see Purple Claw's face. He could just hear his jaws smacking.

"What a nice castle you have," the General said brightly, gobbling his food. "Have you lived here long?"

"Only a few hours," Purple Claw drawled. "And I shall move out after dinner."

"Why are you leaving so soon?" asked the General, who did not know that sand castles get washed away by the tide. Purple Claw did not reply.

"What brings *you* here?" he asked instead, changing the subject.

"I was just taking a little stroll," the General said cagily. Something told him that it would be best not to tell Purple Claw about the treasure.

"The beach is a very dangerous place for a *stroll*," Purple Claw sneered.

"Well, seeing as it was such a nice day, and seeing as I'm only in Mousewall for a week, I thought a stroll would be rather pleasant," the General said nervously.

The conversation was not going at all as conversations should, and he suddenly felt very ill at ease. He had finished his flies, so he decided to ask for directions back to Smugglers' Keep and get straight on his way.

"If you'll excuse me, I really must be getting home, or my friends will be worrying about me," he said, getting up from his pebble. "Perhaps you could be kind enough to direct me back to Smugglers' Keep—"

"*Smugglers' Keep?*" Purple Claw barked, sounding very interested.

"Yes...er...that's where I'm staying, you see—with Lord Seamouse," the General replied. "And...er..." He knew he was saying too much. But he was so confused, he had started to babble. "And...er...now I really must get back. Don't worry if you don't know the way, I'm sure I'll find it. At least I've still got the map—"

"*THE MAP?* What map?" Purple Claw hissed.

"Oh, just a map of the beach, nothing...er...nothing special," the General stammered. "Now if you'll excuse me, it really is time I went."

He stumbled across the room, trying to find the way out. But the smoke was so thick that everything was a haze.

Then suddenly he saw Purple Claw standing just in front of him. He was smiling a fiendish smile, and his eyes were blazing.

"Give me the map," Purple Claw said very slowly, reaching out his paw.

"*NO, I WON'T!*" the General squealed.

"*YES—YOU—WILL!*" Purple Claw snarled. Then all at once the General saw a pistol being pointed at him.

He heard a peal of hideous laughter, then everything went black.

# Chapter Seven

The General woke up feeling very groggy. He looked around in a daze, trying to work out what had happened.

He was lying on the floor of the sand castle, and his clothes were soggy. The fire had gone out, and there was moonlight piercing through the arrow slits.

Suddenly he remembered Purple Claw pointing a pistol at him — and when he felt in his pocket, the map was gone.

"The thief!" he cried. "Just wait till I catch him!"

He tried to get up, but he could feel a sharp pain in his lungs, and his head was throbbing.

Then he noticed a funny smell. He twitched his nose, trying to identify it. But it was so strong it made his nostrils burn. And he could see clouds of green vapor wafting in the air.

The smell hit him again — and all at once, he realized what it was.

"PEPPERMINT GAS!" he yelped. "He's sprayed me with peppermint gas!"

The General staggered to his feet, desperate to get out. He had seen peppermint gas used in the Royal Mouse Army, and he knew it was a terrible thing.

It is a deadly weapon that can knock a mouse out cold, and make his nose turn blue, and his whiskers crinkle. And if a mouse inhales enough of it, his stomach knots, and his kidneys twist, and his lungs sizzle. . . .

So no wonder the General felt alarmed.

He stumbled through the archway and stood outside, taking big gulps of air. Slowly, his head stopped throbbing, and he knew he had escaped in time.

Even so, he felt very wretched.

The mission had gone horribly wrong. He had hoped to

return to Seaview Hollow a hero, carrying Uncle Jeremy's teeth. But instead he had lost the map. Just think how cross Tumtum and Lord Seamouse would be when they found out! And that's if he ever managed to find his way home!

He stood miserably on the drawbridge, gazing at the vast moonlit beach. He had no idea which way to go.

But then suddenly he saw a light high up in the distance — and to his relief he realized that it was the lantern in front of Smugglers' Keep. And below it, he could just make out the pale outline of the steps in the harbor wall.

*Well, at least I'm not lost anymore. That's one good thing*, he thought as he stepped onto the drawbridge.

But then he heard a sudden roar — and all at once a jet of ice-cold water scooped him up and flung him back through the archway.

There was water everywhere. Black water, swirling all around him. Around and around it went, tossing and rolling him across the castle floor.

Then it suddenly gushed away.

The General scrabbled to his feet and ran to an arrow slit. And when he looked down the beach, he saw a sight that froze the blood in his tail—a huge foaming wave, snarling toward him.

In an instant, it reared up over his head and smashed into the castle turret. He ran blindly across the room and stumbled outside onto the drawbridge. The castle was tumbling to the ground, and the moat was rising. And the next moment the bridge was sucked from under him, and the General was plunged into the water.

He thrashed his paws frantically, but the current was battering him in all directions.

"Help!" he cried.

Then a big wave swelled up beneath him and spat him out onto the sand.

He lay there trembling. He felt too weak to move. But he could hear the next wave coming toward him.

With a final burst of strength, he dragged himself to his feet, and staggered toward the harbor wall. Then he started

frantically clambering up the big stone steps as the sea crashed behind him.

Finally, he reached the lane. He was out of danger now. But there was still a voice in his head crying, *Run! Run! Run!* And run he did, as fast as his trembling legs would carry him — into the cottage, and through the kitchen, and across the hall, and up the stairs. . . .

He didn't stop until he reached Seaview Hollow.

The Nutmouses and Lord Seamouse were sitting in the drawing room when they heard his exhausted *Rat! Tat! Tat!* on the front door.

"He's back!" they shouted, racing into the hall.

It was long past midnight, but they had all been much too worried to go to bed. And they were so relieved to see the General again that at first they forgot to be upset.

"You're soaking wet!" Nutmeg cried. "Now sit down by the fire, and we'll find you some nice dry clothes to wear."

Everyone made a great fuss over him. Lord Seamouse lent him a pair of pajamas, and Tumtum lent him a pair of slippers, and Nutmeg hung up his suit to dry and warmed up a big slice of pie for his supper.

They could see he was half-starved. So they waited until he had finished eating before the questions began.

"Where have you been?" Tumtum asked finally.

The General scowled. Normally he loved boasting about his adventures. But he felt that what had happened today did not show him off in a very good light.

"We know you stole the map," Tumtum said when he didn't answer. "Really, General, what on earth were you thinking? You must know there's no point in trying to find the treasure yourself. You could never carry it all back from the cave."

"I just wanted to find Uncle Jeremy's teeth," the General replied sulkily. "The children can go and get all the rest. But *I* want to find the famous missing teeth, and bring them home all by myself, and get my picture in the *Mouse Times*. And I will! So there!"

"Oh, no you won't!" Tumtum retorted. "We will return the map to Lucy's bedside table tonight. This is their treasure hunt, and you've no right to interfere!"

The General crossed his arms grumpily.

Everyone thought he was being very silly.

"We might as well take the map back now, then we can all go to bed," Nutmeg said.

"Good idea," Tumtum agreed, getting up from his chair. "Come on then, General—give it back."

The General squirmed and turned very red.

There was a tense silence. Everyone was thinking the same thing.

"You didn't . . . you didn't *lose it*, did you?" Lord Seamouse asked eventually.

The General grunted.

"Oh, how could you be such a fool?" Tumtum cried. "You knew it was the only copy in the whole world!"

"Oh, leave me alone. I didn't lose it!" the General shouted. "IT WAS STOLEN!"

"*Stolen?*" Lord Seamouse gulped.

"Yes, STOLEN!" the General said indignantly. "I met a horrible villain on the beach, who lured me into his beastly sand castle, then poisoned me with peppermint gas, then stole the

156

map while I was out for the count! But just you wait. I'll teach that rascal to mess with *me*!"

Lord Seamouse had started to quake.

"Wh...wh...what was his name?" he stammered.

"Purple Claw," the General replied. "Very silly name if you ask me — silly name for a — "

But then there was a loud crash. It was Lord Seamouse, fainting on the floor.

## Chapter Eight

Lord Seamouse was soon revived with a cold cloth and a glass of water.

But he was in a terrible state.

"Purple Claw! Oh me, oh my! Oh no, oh no!" he kept saying.

Everyone tried to calm him, but he wasn't making any sense.

Tumtum and Nutmeg wondered who Purple Claw could possibly be that his name had such a terrible effect.

"Was he very frightening?" they asked the General.

"*I* certainly wasn't frightened of him," the General lied. "I don't know what Lord Seamouse is making such a fuss about."

"Oh, but you don't know anything!" Lord Seamouse spluttered. "Purple Claw is the biggest villain in all of Mousewall. Everyone trembles when they hear his name! He lurks in sand castles, ambushing any mouse who comes near. He jumps out and says, 'BOO!' and steals your picnic basket and your fishing nets. He'll even steal your swimming trunks, if he likes the look of them! And oh, woe betide you if you make an enemy of him! He'll appear at your mouse hole in the middle of the night and drag you from your bed, kicking and shrieking...then he'll take you to the beach and throw you to the sea horses!"

"What an awful-sounding fellow," Tumtum said. Nutmeg was so alarmed that as a precaution she went and bolted the front door.

"I've seen him lurking around in Uncle Jeremy's garden, watching me come and go," Lord Seamouse quivered. "He must have suspected that I knew where the teeth were hidden. He'd give his front fangs for them. He knows how much gold he'd get from the tooth fairies for a full set of milk teeth! If he got his claws on them he'd become so rich there would be no end to his powers. He'd build himself castles and battleships, and he'd employ his own private army to rob and steal for him, and every mouse in Mousewall would live in dread."

"Then we must make sure the children find the treasure first!" Nutmeg cried.

"But we can't stop Purple Claw now!" Lord Seamouse trembled. "Why, if he finds out we've been plotting against him, he'll...he'll..."

"Oh, nonsense!" the General said sharply, wishing Lord Seamouse would be a little more brave. "We can't let that old tramp frighten us off. Besides, he'll never be able to get across the Rock Pool without a boat."

"Oh, Purple Claw can get anywhere," Lord Seamouse replied. "He's got SPECIAL POWERS!"

"Well, he's still only a mouse. He'll be no match for Arthur and Lucy," Nutmeg said firmly. "They'll scare him off all right."

Lord Seamouse looked a little reassured by this. He supposed even Purple Claw might be frightened when he saw the size of *them*.

"I will write the children a letter, asking them to go back

to Stargazer first thing in the morning," Nutmeg said. "They already know which rock the treasure's hidden in, so they shouldn't need the map."

"But what if they can't find the right cave?" Tumtum asked. "They've already spent a whole morning looking for it. And Stargazer's huge—it must contain a thousand nooks and crannies."

"Tell them to search near the peak," Lord Seamouse said. "Whoever stole the treasure's sure to have hidden it as high up in the rock as possible. When the tide comes in, the caves lower down the rock face are completely submerged—no mouse in his right mind would have hidden it there."

"Good idea," Nutmeg said. "That should narrow down their search!"

Lord Seamouse found her a piece of paper, and she quickly scribbled the children a message, telling them exactly what to do.

"Arthur and Lucy won't let Purple Claw get the better of *them!*" she said.

When the children woke up the next morning, they found Nutmeg's letter:

> *Dear Arthur and Lucy,*
>
> *Your map has been stolen by a wicked villain called Purple Claw, who is determined to find the treasure before you do and use it to make himself rich and powerful. But we must not let him! You must return to Stargazer at once, my dears, and resume your search. I am told the treasure is most likely to be hidden close to the rock's peak, where the tide cannot reach it. But be careful how you go, for Purple Claw will be lurking. Try not to arouse his suspicions. Now hurry, my dears. For time is running out.*
>
> *Love,*
>
> *Nutmeg*

The children read it with astonishment.

"*Purple Claw*," Arthur said quietly, thinking it a very strange name. "Who do you think he is?"

"Well, if he's anything like his name suggests, then he'll have purple claws," Lucy replied. "Maybe he's a rat!"

Arthur shuddered. Mice were one thing, but rats were quite another. Once a gang of them had kidnapped Nutmeg and kept her prisoner on the farm pond. If it weren't for Arthur and Lucy, she might never have escaped. From everything he had heard, rats were a very nasty breed.

He looked at his watch. It was nearly eight o'clock.

"Come on! Whoever Purple Claw is, we'd better hurry if we're going to get there before he does," he said. They quickly got dressed, then as soon as they had finished breakfast they ran outside.

But when they saw the beach they both groaned. The sea was lapping against the rocks, and the pool was completely hidden.

"Well, we can't look for the treasure now," Arthur said.

"Is the tide coming in or going out?" Lucy asked.

"Uncle Jeremy will know," Arthur said. They ran back inside to ask him.

"Let's see," Uncle Jeremy said, looking at his watch. "Yes, it'll be on its way out now."

"How long till it goes down below the rocks?" the children asked impatiently.

Uncle Jeremy looked at them curiously. They had a whole week to play on the beach, so he wondered why they were in such a hurry.

"I'd give it an hour or two," he said. "Now don't look so glum. The beach will still be there." Then he disappeared behind his newspaper again.

The children paced restlessly around the cottage, rushing to the window every five minutes to look out. It seemed as if the tide would never go out. But eventually it did.

"Come on!" Lucy said, and they rushed into the hall.

"Don't forget your backpack," Mrs. Blythe said, appearing from the kitchen. "I've packed a water bottle for you, and some cookies."

"Thank you!" Lucy said, taking the bag and tugging it onto

her shoulder. Then they ran outside and raced down to the beach. Arthur was carrying his toy speedboat. "Why did you bring that?" Lucy asked.

"So we can pretend we're playing with it," he replied. "Nutmeg said we should try not to make Purple Claw suspicious. Well, if he sees us playing with our boat in the Rock Pool, he'll think we're just messing around, instead of looking for treasure."

"Good idea," Lucy said—for they certainly didn't want Purple Claw getting wind of what they were up to.

When they reached the rocks, they scrambled up to the pool, and Lucy slung the backpack onto the ground.

"According to Nutmeg, the cave must be right up there," Arthur said, pointing to the top of Stargazer.

"*Don't point*," Lucy whispered. "He might be watching!"

There was no one on the beach, and there was not a mouse or rat to be seen. But Lucy had an uncomfortable feeling, as though they were being followed.

She made Arthur feel anxious, too.

"Come on, let's pretend we're playing with the boat," he

said. He knelt down beside the Rock Pool and placed it on the water. Then Lucy knelt beside him and pretended to be playing, too. But she kept glancing over her shoulder. It was a horrible feeling—but whoever Purple Claw was, she felt sure he could see them.

And indeed he could. For Purple Claw was crouched behind a pebble on the far side of the pool, watching their every move. He was dressed in a black wet suit, and he was holding his sailboard.

Purple Claw wasn't fooled by the boat. From the moment Arthur pointed up to the rock, he guessed that the children were after the treasure, too.

"Curse them!" he hissed.

He could see the Grotto on the far side of the pool, and he knew from the map that it was where he must get to. He had been about to slip into the water and start windsurfing toward it—but then the children had appeared.

He crouched very still, watching Arthur and Lucy with

gritted fangs. If he was going to reach the treasure first, he would have to get rid of them. And there were all sorts of wicked thoughts whirring through his mind.

But Purple Claw was not the only mouse present.

Though he did not know it, Tumtum and Nutmeg and Lord Seamouse and General Marchmouse were also there—hiding inside the pocket of Lucy's backpack.

It had been Nutmeg who had insisted that they come. She knew Purple Claw could be no match for the children. But she wanted to be there just in case.

But Purple Claw was so well hidden behind his pebble, the other mice hadn't spotted him.

The pocket was quite a squash. They were all standing tight together, with their heads poked over the side. The General was scouring the rocks with his field glasses. He felt sure Purple Claw must be there somewhere. He had brought his slingshot along and was looking forward to pelting him with an ink cartridge.

"Can you see him?" Lord Seamouse asked, not for the first time.

"No. Still no sign of him," the General said — but then suddenly he caught sight of Arthur's boat, and he felt his heart throb.

It was a deep crimson, with a fat wooden steering wheel, and a motor as big as a matchbox.

Oh, what a golden opportunity this was!

The General had almost given up hope of finding the teeth by himself — for he didn't dare make another attempt to cross the pool. But in a boat such as that he would be quite safe. He could zoom into the Grotto so fast the Crabby Crab would hardly see him coming!

It was a heavenly plan! But he knew he must act fast.

He lowered his field glasses and gave the others a sly look. Then he suddenly sprang out of the backpack pocket and started hurtling off across the rock.

"Come back! They'll see you!" Tumtum shouted.

But the General didn't care.

He made straight for the edge of the pool, where the children were sitting. Then he tore over Arthur's lap and leaped down into the speedboat.

"What was that?" Arthur cried, looking around in astonishment.

The General flung himself onto the driver's seat and turned the control switch to ON. There was a sudden *Vroom!* and the boat sped out across the water.

"Stop!" the children cried, trying to grab it. But it was already out of reach. Faster and faster it went, its propellers thrashing through the slime.

The children watched in astonishment. And as the boat veered around to enter the cave, they saw a mouse in a green suit whooping at the wheel.

# Chapter Nine

The boat sped into the Grotto. Then it gave a last *Vroom!* of its motor and disappeared from sight.

Purple Claw, who was watching from behind his pebble, stamped his feet with rage.

He had left the General to drown in a sand castle. However did he escape?

Purple Claw knew he must move fast, or the General would reach the teeth first. He would have to windsurf after him at once — and it didn't matter if the children saw him!

He slunk out from his hiding place and crept to the edge of the pool. But just as he was lowering his sailboard into the water, he saw something moving in the slime. Then all at once the tip of a pincer appeared . . . and then out peeked a big goggling eye!

It was the Crabby Crab! And when he caught sight of the children, he sank back to the bottom of the pool. But he had given Purple Claw a terrible fright.

"Eek!" he cried, reeling backward. He didn't dare windsurf across the pool now. Not with a pink monster lurking underwater!

But then how was he to reach the Grotto?

He needed a plan. And his eyes went black as he started plotting.

Tumtum and Nutmeg and Lord Seamouse, who were watching from the backpack pocket, had also seen the General disappear.

And they were furious.

"How dare he!" Tumtum raged. "He promised he wouldn't interfere again!"

"Oh, promises, promises! The General's never thought much of those," Nutmeg groaned.

"Well, we can't stop him now," Lord Seamouse said. "We'll just have to hope that Purple Claw doesn't follow him."

"Oh, I do wish Arthur and Lucy would buck up and find the treasure! Then we could all go home!" Nutmeg cried.

But the children were still standing beside the Rock Pool—staring at the little black hole into which the boat had disappeared.

"That mouse must have been Purple Claw!" Lucy said. "Oh, we are stupid! Nutmeg warned us to look out for him— and now we've gone and let him steal our boat!"

"We must get it back!" Arthur cried.

But the only way to reach the Grotto was to wade into the pool. And the water looked so dark and slimy that neither child dared to.

Besides, the entrance to the Grotto was very small—if the boat had gone in far, they would never be able to fish it out.

"Come on!" Lucy said. "As long as we can find the cave, we'll still get to the treasure first!"

"All right," Arthur said, scrambling to his feet. "I'll climb up and look for it."

He ran around the side of the pool and started pulling himself up the rock face, until he could reach the top. He hugged the rock with one hand, and started groping around with the other.

Presently, his hand found a small opening in the rock. "There's a cave here!" he shouted. "This might be it!"

Lucy watched impatiently as he moved his hand around inside — but all he found was an old water bottle. He tossed it down to her in disgust. Then he felt all around the rest of the rock. But there were no more openings. And the top of the rock was covered in a thick blanket of moss.

Eventually, he gave up and jumped back down.

"Well, now we've looked everywhere," he said glumly. "The treasure must not be here after all."

The children looked at the rocks in dismay. If the treasure wasn't in Stargazer, then wherever could it be?

## Chapter Ten

It was pitch-black in the Grotto. All the General could see was the pale beam of his flashlight, slipping over the walls.

He turned down his engine and inched the boat forward, searching for the Secret Tunnel.

The deeper he went, the colder the cave became. He shivered and rubbed his paws on the steering wheel to keep warm. Then all of a sudden there was a pool of green light—and to his surprise, he saw a lantern hanging from the wall.

Below the lantern, there was a small opening in the rock. And beside it, carved into the rock in big rough letters, was written:

"Hurrah!" the General cried.

He chugged toward it and tied his boat to a thin sliver of rock jutting from the wall. Then he clambered up into the passage.

The tunnel twisted and turned, and got fatter and thinner, and colder and damper—and in places it was so steep that the General had to clamber along on all fours.

Eventually, he came to a big cave, the size of a shoe box. On the other side of the cave, there was a flight of stairs cut into the rock. He climbed up—but when he got to the top, there was just a brick wall.

"Drat," he said, thinking he had reached a dead end.

But just as he was about to turn back down the stairs, he noticed a thin ribbon of light on the floor.

And when he shone his flashlight over the wall, he saw to his astonishment that there was a door cut into the rock. It didn't have a bell. There was just a rusty iron latch and a bolt that had been left drawn.

He lifted the latch and gave the door a push. It felt very stiff, as if it hadn't been used for a long time. And when it opened, there was a flood of golden light.

The General stepped inside and gave a loud gulp. He was in a cave lit by a chandelier and filled with the most sumptuous treasures. There were paintings and tapestries, and silver candlesticks, and four-poster beds with velvet curtains. And there was a big enamel bath, and a toilet with a pink seat! And there were chests full of fancy jugs and plates, and a dining room table with a china swan on top!

General Marchmouse was astonished—he had never seen such luxuries.

No wonder Lord Seamouse was so anxious to get everything back.

But the General wasn't interested in the furniture. It was Uncle Jeremy's teeth he had come for. He started rummaging through the chests, pulling out the jugs and plates and cups and candlesticks, determined to find them.

Then he noticed a rusty candy tin in the corner of the cave, with the words FRUIT PASTILLES written on it. He scuttled over to it and pried off the lid . . . and there they were — a whole set of fat white milk teeth, shining like pearls.

The General gasped. Just think how much the tooth fairies would pay for teeth such as these! It was hardly surprising Purple Claw was so keen to get his paws on them.

But he was too late now!

The General quickly pressed the lid back on the tin and heaved it up onto his shoulders.

He wanted to get away as quickly as possible and show off his amazing discovery. He couldn't wait to tell the *Mouse Times* that he had solved The Case of the Missing Teeth — when every other mouse in Mousewall had failed!

But as he was staggering to the door, he suddenly saw some bright beads of light coming from the back of the cave — and

when he looked more closely he saw that there was a dark green curtain hanging there.

He put down the tin and walked over to it, wondering what was on the other side. And when he touched the curtain, he found to his surprise that it was made of moss. It was so thick he had to push his way through it with both paws—and when he came out on the other side he let out a cry.

For suddenly he was outside again! He was standing at the mouth of the cave, right at the top of Stargazer—and below him the rock fell away in a steep cliff. He could see the Rock Pool far below him, and the gulls wheeling in the air above.

He was so high up he felt quite giddy.

He crouched down on all fours, for he was frightened of losing his balance. Then he took up his field glasses and peered down the cliff. Arthur and Lucy had gone. But he wondered if Tumtum and the others had stayed behind.

He looked all around the beach, as far as he could see. But there was no sign of them. He supposed they must have gone back to Smugglers' Keep with the children.

Then he noticed a big sand castle, just in front of the rocks, with a red flag flying from the turret. He twisted his lens to bring it into focus and then his heart gave a sudden jolt.

Purple Claw was standing in the watchtower with a telescope — peering straight at him.

## Chapter Eleven

The General stumbled back through the curtain, shaken to the core. He knew Purple Claw had seen him. And now he would be lying in wait, ready to ambush him as he made his way home with the teeth.

The situation was hopeless. The General would never be able to get past him.

He paced anxiously around the cave, wondering what to do.

Then all of a sudden he heard a rap on the door.

The General froze. It must be Purple Claw! But how could he have been so quick?

The General grabbed a chair and pressed himself against the wall, waiting to clobber him as he came in.

As the door opened, the General heard some muffled voices on the other side. *He must have accomplices,* he thought anxiously.

He tightened his grip on the chair, ready to bash the first mouse who appeared. But when he saw who it was, he gave a cry of relief.

"Tumtum! Nutmeg! Lord Seamouse! What are *you* doing here?" he gasped.

There was a lot of explaining to be done. But when Tumtum and Nutmeg saw all the treasure, they were too astonished to speak.

Seaview Manor must have been the grandest dollhouse in the world!

Lord Seamouse became quite emotional. He wandered around the cave in a delighted trance, gazing at his beloved possessions. He had feared he might never see them again. But here they all were — and everything intact! Some of the furniture looked a little dusty. But it was nothing that a good polishing wouldn't fix.

"Just think!" he said tearfully. "Soon everything will be

returned to Seaview Manor, and I'll be able to move back into my old home again!"

The General looked sulky — for despite his grand adventure, no one was making a fuss of him. "I got here first!" he said stubbornly.

Tumtum turned to him savagely. He had been so overawed by the sight of the treasure that for a moment he had forgotten how angry he was. But he had remembered now. "I know you did, and I've a good mind to box your ears!" he said. "We need Arthur and Lucy to carry this treasure back to Smugglers' Keep — we'll never get it home on our own. But then you try and mess everything up! First you steal the map, then the children's boat. You should be ashamed of yourself! But if you think you can spoil everything, you can think again. We've come to take you home!"

The General huffed. "How did you come after me without a boat?" he asked. "You're lucky the Crabby Crab didn't catch you."

"It was thanks to the crab that we got here," Tumtum replied. "After you went into the Grotto, we climbed out of the backpack and came down to the pool to see if we could call you back. Then the Crabby Crab poked his head out of the water. And the four of us got talking, and it turned out that he's not crabby at all. Most delightful fellow, in fact. And when we explained why we were there, he told us all to hop onto his back—then he carried us to the Secret Tunnel."

"Huh," the General said. "I wish he'd been as helpful with me."

"And he said that if Purple Claw tries to cross the pool, he'll gobble him up!" Nutmeg added. "So we don't have to worry about him following us up here."

Tumtum frowned. He was looking at the walls of the cave. "How will the children ever find the cave from the outside?" he asked. "Look, it's completely enclosed!"

"No, it's not," the General replied. He walked to the back of the cave and pulled aside a corner of the moss, so they could see outside.

Everyone was astonished. The cave was very well hidden. No wonder the children hadn't found it yet.

"Keep still," the General warned them. "When I went out

earlier, Purple Claw saw me. He was lurking in that sand castle down there."

"Oh, no!" Tumtum said. "I hope he doesn't give us any trouble on the way home."

"It's all right, I know another way we can go," Lord Seamouse said. "We can cut up beside the rocks, then creep along the bottom of the harbor wall. That way we won't have to pass the sand castle."

"Good," Tumtum said. "Now come on, we'd better get going. We've still got a long walk back to Smugglers' Keep."

They all made for the door — except the General, who was hovering by the tin of teeth.

The children could fetch the rest of the treasure — but he didn't see why he should leave the teeth behind. He could carry them home himself — they weren't too heavy. Then he could tell the *Mouse Times* that it was he who had found them, and imagine what a fuss there would be!

"Come on, General — hurry up," Tumtum said impatiently.

"I'm bringing these with me!" the General said stubbornly, hoisting the tin onto his back.

"Don't be ridiculous," Tumtum said. "If Purple Claw sees us carrying a treasure chest across the beach, he's sure to come and ambush us!"

"Oh, forget Purple Claw!" the General snapped.

It was blowing up into quite an argument. But then all of a sudden there was a huge roar outside the cave.

"It's a bird!" Nutmeg cried.

"That's not a bird," the General said. "*That's a plane!*"

"Duck!" Tumtum cried.

At that moment, a fierce blast of wind swept open the curtain. And as the mice looked out in horror, they saw a toy airplane swooping toward the cave.

They flattened themselves against the wall, for it was coming straight at them. It was so close they could see into the cockpit. And what a surprise they got! For there was Purple Claw, grinning horribly as he clung to the joystick.

# Chapter Twelve

Purple Claw's plane plowed into the cave. It landed with a
ferocious bang. One of the engines exploded, and there
was smoke billowing down the wings.

The plane had taken a terrible battering. Everyone wondered if Purple Claw had survived — but then the roof of the
cockpit flipped open, and out he stepped.

He looked very calm, despite his crash landing.

"How do you do?" he purred, peeling off his goggles.

"You are outnumbered, Purple Claw! Now get out of here
or I'll make you sorry!" the General shouted in his most menac-
ing voice.

He stepped forward, baring his fists — but Purple Claw

just sneered. Then he reached into his cape and whipped out his peppermint gun.

"Face the wall, with your paws behind your backs!" he barked.

And they all did, including General Marchmouse — for even the bravest mouse does what he's told when someone's pointing a peppermint gun at him.

Then Purple Claw tied them up with cotton, pulling it so tight it burned their skin.

"You rogue! You won't get away with this!" the General fumed.

"Oh, yes I will!" Purple Claw said, giving him a push. When all the prisoners were bound, he started upturning the chests and cupboards, searching for the teeth. And when he finally found the candy tin and pried open the lid, his heart gave a surge.

"Ha! Ha! Just think how much gold the tooth fairies will give me for all of these!" he cried. "Oh, what a rich and power-ful villain I will be!"

In his mind's eye, he saw the life he would lead — a life of banquets, and fine clothes, and feather beds. "I'll buy a yacht!" he shrieked, clapping his paws in delight. "And I'll build myself a palace in the dunes, and I'll employ an army of field mice to do all my robbing and thieving!"

The idea was so glorious it made him shiver. But this was no time for dreaming. He knew he must get out fast, in case those tiresome children came back.

He stuffed his gun back into his holster and heaved the tin onto his shoulders.

"Goodbye, my dears!" he said mockingly — then he staggered through the door, and slammed it shut behind him.

A moment later, the mice heard the bolts being clicked shut on the other side.

"He's locked us in!" the General fumed.

They were trapped!

"Come on, let's get these ropes off. We can't do anything with our paws tied," Tumtum said. But Purple Claw had secured the knots very tightly.

"I'll try and gnaw through them," Nutmeg said. She leaned down and started nibbling at Tumtum's ropes.

194

*Nibble! Nibble! Nibble!*

*Chomp! Chomp! Chomp!*

On and on she gnawed, until her jaws ached.

The others watched tensely. Eventually, Tumtum's ropes fell free.

The others cheered. Then Tumtum quickly undid their paws, too. They all rubbed their wrists, for the cotton had left red welts on their skin.

"Come on! Let's try and smash open the door," the General cried. "Purple Claw will still be in the tunnel—we can catch up with him and spring on him from behind!"

Everyone agreed that the scoundrel must be stopped.

But though they all kicked and battered the door together, and rammed it with a dresser, it wouldn't budge.

"We'll never escape!" Nutmeg said tearfully.

They felt helpless. With every second that passed, Purple Claw would be creeping farther down the Secret Tunnel toward Arthur's boat.

"We must stop him!" the General cried.

Everyone racked their brains, wondering what to do.

"I wish we could get a message to the children," Tumtum said. "Then we could tell them to come back to the Rock Pool and catch Purple Claw red-handed when he comes out of the Grotto!"

"Oh, that would serve him right!" the General said.

It was a wonderful idea. But of course it would never work, for how could they get a message to the children when they were stuck up here in the cave?

"If only Purple Claw's plane weren't smashed to bits, then one of us could fly back to Smugglers' Keep!" Nutmeg said.

The General gave a start. He had been so busy battering the door, he hadn't thought about the plane.

He turned and looked at it very carefully. Was it *really* as badly damaged as all that?

It was still belching smoke, and the wings were dented. But the propellers had survived, and the cockpit looked intact. He peered inside and saw that the fuel gauge was showing half-full.

The General's whiskers started to quiver. "She'll fly for me!" he said.

# Chapter Thirteen

The Nutmouses and Lord Seamouse were still standing by the door, discussing what to do.

"I say, where's the General?" Tumtum asked suddenly.

Then all at once there was a deafening roar. And when they looked around they saw the airplane tearing across the cave, with General Marchmouse shrieking in the cockpit. There was smoke choking the wings, and the engine was spluttering.

Everyone ran for cover.

"*BRAKE!*" Tumtum shouted.

"*STOP!*" Nutmeg screeched.

But there was no stopping him now.

"Clear the skies!" the General cried. "I'm taking off!" Then he tore into the curtain.

Everything went black as the moss slapped over the windshield. Then the plane slipped over the edge of the cave and plunged into the air.

"I'm flying!" the General shouted, giggling with glee.

But when he looked out of the window he gave a loud yelp. He wasn't flying. He was sinking like a stone! And all he could see were vast black rocks, spinning all around him.

He turned to the control panel and started yanking the knobs. But the plane kept falling.

"Help!" he cried.

He saw a green lever beside the joystick, labeled THROTTLE.

He grabbed it with both paws and wrenched it toward him.

There was a violent shudder, and he felt his seat vibrate. Then the engine went *VROOOOOM!* and suddenly the nose of the plane flipped up and the craft soared skyward.

The General gave a whoop. He was going higher and higher, wheeling through the air like a gull.

"I am Lord of the Skies!" he cried, thumping his paw on the roof.

When he looked down, he could see Tumtum and Nutmeg and Lord Seamouse, watching him in terror from the mouth of the cave.

And how he showed off!

He looped the loop, and he did a figure eight, then a figure nine. . . .

But then suddenly he saw an enormous shape looming toward him. It had white wings and an orange nose.

The General gulped. It was a seagull, coming straight at him!

He yanked the joystick, trying to steer out of its path. But it was too late . . . and a moment later the bird thwacked into the cockpit.

The plane batted backward like a football and started plummeting from the sky.

The General peered through the window in terror.

He could see the beach below him, spinning nearer and nearer . . . then there was a sudden *Smack! Bang!* as the plane crashed into a sand castle.

The General lay in the cockpit, too dazed to move. Everything was swimming. All he could see were stars.

Then he smelled burning. "Fire!" he cried.

He wrenched open the door and dragged himself out. Then he started racing frantically through the sand. He saw a shell in front of him and ducked behind it. And the next moment there was a huge blast, as the plane exploded in a torrent of flames.

The General cowered there for a moment, feeling very shaken. He fished a handkerchief from his pocket and wiped his brow. What an adventurous day it had been! And it wasn't over yet.

He still had to get a message to the children. And if they were to come back in time to catch Purple Claw, then he didn't have a moment to lose.

He dragged himself to his feet and stumbled on through the sand. Then he clambered up the steps, shot across the lane, and wriggled into Smugglers' Keep under the garden door.

He crept through the kitchen, into the hall. He could hear voices coming from the dining room, and when he peeked

around the door, he saw Arthur and Lucy sitting at the table, finishing their lunch.

He quickly searched around the hall for something to write on. Then he saw a small table against the far wall, with a telephone cord dangling down to the floor. He scrambled up it, and when he reached the tabletop he found a pad of white paper and a jar of pens.

He pushed the jar over, then he pulled out a pen and wrestled off the cap. He tore a piece of paper from the pad and, holding the pen with both arms, he scrawled out his orders:

*ATTN: Arthur and Lucy Mildew*

*Your uncle's childhood teeth have been stolen by Purple Claw, and he intends to sell them to the tooth fairies and make himself rich and powerful. But if you do exactly as I say, you can stop him.*

*You must proceed at once to the Rock Pool and wait for Purple Claw to emerge from the cave in your speedboat. As soon as you see the boat coming, swoop down and grab it. Then the teeth will be yours! As for Purple Claw — he will*

*be yours, too. Do what you wish with him. A cage with*

*thick bars might be the best answer.*

*Yours,*

*General Marchmouse*

When he finished writing, the General folded the note in half and clenched it between his teeth. Then he scrambled down to the floor and crept into the dining room.

Mrs. Blythe had appeared now and was standing beside Lucy, spooning a second helping of rice pudding into her bowl.

The General was in such a hurry, he did not even wait until she had gone. He shot straight across the carpet and scurried up the tablecloth. Then he leaped over the sugar dish and dropped his letter beside Lucy's bowl.

Mrs. Blythe shrieked and dropped her spoon with a clang.

"It's that green mouse again!" Arthur cried as the General darted back to the floor. Arthur leaped from his chair, trying to see where he went. But the General was gone.

# Chapter Fourteen

**M**rs. Blythe shrieked and squawked and made a terrible fuss.

Uncle Jeremy had been in the drawing room, answering a telephone call. When he heard the noise, he came hurrying into the dining room.

"What's going on?" he asked.

"It was a mouse!" she cried. "A mouse wearing *clothes!*"

"Don't be silly, Mrs. Blythe. Mice don't wear clothes," Uncle Jeremy said.

"Well, I'm telling you, this one did!" Mrs. Blythe replied. "Ask the children. They saw it!"

"Did you?" Uncle Jeremy asked, looking somewhat bewildered.

Arthur and Lucy went red. They *had* seen it—and now Lucy was clutching the General's note in her hand. But they didn't want to have to start explaining everything to the grown-ups.

"There was a mouse," Lucy said. "It ran across the table. Then it ran off again."

"And was it wearing clothes?" Uncle Jeremy asked, clearly thinking this was all very silly.

"I . . . er . . . I didn't notice," Lucy mumbled.

"Neither did I," Arthur said.

"But it *was*," Mrs. Blythe cried. "I tell you, it *was!*"

Uncle Jeremy gave Mrs. Blythe a kindly look. He wondered if it was the hot weather that had made her so muddled.

"Well, I can assure you, if I see it I'll send it running!" he said. But Mrs. Blythe did not look at all reassured.

As soon as lunch was finished, Arthur and Lucy ran upstairs to read their letter. The General's writing was much bigger than Nutmeg's, so they did not need a magnifying glass. Arthur sat next to Lucy on the bed while she read it out loud.

"So there we were thinking the mouse in the green suit was Purple Claw—but he's on *our* side," Arthur said.

"And he's a general!" Lucy said in astonishment.

The children had never heard of the Royal Mouse Army, so they hadn't known that mice could be generals.

"Do you think Purple Claw is a mouse, too?" Arthur asked—for the General's letter hadn't made it clear.

"He must be, if he's small enough to fit in the boat," Lucy said.

"Come on!" Arthur said, jumping up from the bed. "Whoever he is, we'd better go and catch him!"

"We'll need something to put him in," Lucy said. "We should take a cookie tin."

"We needn't bother. We can put him in a fishing net," Arthur said.

"All right," Lucy agreed. So they ran downstairs and grabbed their fishing nets from the hall, then they raced back to the beach.

Tumtum and Nutmeg and Lord Seamouse, meanwhile, were looking out anxiously from the mouth of the cave.

They had seen the General's plane crash into the sand castle. And they had seen him clamber out of the wreckage and start scurrying back toward Smugglers' Keep.

And when they saw Arthur and Lucy charging back across the sand, they knew he must have gotten his message to them and warned them about what was going on.

"Oh, hooray. They're back!" Nutmeg cried.

"And look! They've brought nets to catch Purple Claw!" Lord Seamouse said gleefully.

They couldn't wait to see what happened.

"Hurry, hurry!" they all cried, fearing the children might not reach the pool in time.

The mice watched as Arthur and Lucy scrambled up onto the rocks and stood waiting by the pool with their nets.

But they waited and waited — and still Purple Claw didn't come. The Rock Pool was quite still. There was nothing stirring, not even a dragonfly.

"Do you think he's escaped already?" Lucy asked.

"He can't have, otherwise the boat would be here," Arthur said.

The mice craned over the ledge, trying to see what was going on. It seemed like ages since Purple Claw had left the cave. He should have reached the Grotto by now, and found the boat. They wondered why he was taking so long.

Then suddenly Tumtum noticed Lucy looking their way.

"Keep still!" he hissed.

But it was too late. Lucy had seen them moving out of the corner of her eye, and now she was staring straight at them.

"Look!" she cried. Then Arthur saw them, too—three little mice high up on the rock, dressed in smart summer clothes! The children stared at them in astonishment.

"However did they get up there?" Lucy said.

"They must have come out from behind that green plant," Arthur replied. "Maybe that's where the cave is. I'm going to take a look."

"Oh, do be careful," Lucy said. "They might bite!"

But Arthur was already scrabbling up the rock.

"Quick, get inside!" Tumtum said. And the mice all ran back through the curtain, into the cave.

Arthur pulled himself up slowly, gripping the rock with

both hands. When he was about three feet off the ground he found a little groove to tuck his feet into. He hugged one arm around the rock to keep his balance. Then he reached out his other arm and pushed his hand into the moss.

It was thick and slimy. But when he pressed his hand all the way through, he could feel a hole on the other side.

"There's a cave here all right!" he shouted down to Lucy.

"Is there anything in it?" she asked excitedly.

"Hang on," he said, pushing his hand in deeper.

He stretched out his fingers and groped them around the floor.

Tumtum and Nutmeg and Lord Seamouse pressed themselves against the wall, watching in terror as the huge, pink hand edged closer and closer.

"Quick! Let's hide over there in the wardrobe!" Tumtum whispered.

They jumped over Arthur's thumb and ran toward the wardrobe. They all squeezed in together, then Tumtum pulled the doors shut tight.

"Shhh!" he whispered. "Keep very still!"

Arthur pushed his hand deeper into the cave. Then suddenly his fingers bumped into something solid. It felt like wood. He grabbed it in his fist and pulled it out.

"It's a wardrobe!" he cried.

"Let's see!" Lucy said.

He passed it down to her, and she looked at it in astonishment. It was the prettiest piece of dollhouse furniture she had ever seen. The wood was painted pale blue, and the knobs were made of tiny pearls.

It felt very heavy. *I wonder if there's anything inside*, she thought. She tried to pull the door open, but it was stuck—Tumtum had locked it from the inside.

Arthur turned and reached back into the cave.

"There's tons more!" he said excitedly, fishing out a four-poster bed.

Lucy put the wardrobe on the ground. And as she reached up to take the bed from Arthur, the door squeaked open, and Lord Seamouse and Tumtum and Nutmeg crept out.

"Come on! Let's hide here," Tumtum said, leading them behind a fat gray pebble.

They crouched behind it, watching as Arthur pulled more and more treasures from the cave.

"Here's a bathtub...and a piano....And look! There's even a Ping-Pong table!" he cried.

He passed each item down to Lucy, who packed them into her fishing net. She could hardly wait to take everything back to Seaview Manor. Just think how grand it would look!

"That's everything," Arthur said eventually, when he had explored the last inch of the cave.

"What about the mice?" Lucy asked. "I wonder where they disappeared to."

"They must have escaped somehow. I bet the rock's full of secret tunnels," Arthur said.

He clambered down, then the children stood by the Rock Pool, admiring all the lovely things they had found.

But there was still no sign of the boat.

"Where can it be?" Arthur said.

"*Shhh!*" Lucy said suddenly. "What's that?"

The children both crouched by the pool and listened. They could hear a rumbling noise coming from somewhere deep

inside the rock. It was very faint at first. But then it got louder and louder, until it became a *Vroom! Vroom! Vroom!*

"It's the boat! He's coming!" Arthur whispered. He grabbed his fishing net, then they both waited by the pool, keeping very still.

"He won't get past *us*!" Lucy said.

# Chapter Fifteen

Purple Claw shivered with glee—for his job was almost done.

He had trudged all the way down the Secret Tunnel, lugging the tin of teeth on his shoulders. The tin was very heavy, and it had been a terrible slog. So imagine his joy when he finally reached the Grotto and found the speedboat tied to the wall.

He heaved the tin down into the boat, then he jumped in and undid the mooring rope.

He shone his flashlight over the control panel and pressed the knob marked ON. The engine spluttered, then the boat slowly pulled out onto the water. Purple Claw chugged forward until he could see the big arch of sunlight at the mouth of the Grotto.

He pointed the boat toward it. Then he tightened his grip on the steering wheel and slammed his paw on the accelerator.

The engine roared. The propeller spun. Then the boat reared up its nose and shot forward like a bullet.

"No one can stop me now!" Purple Claw cried as he sped into the sunlight.

The boat skimmed across the Rock Pool—*Buong! Buong! Buong!*—with seaweed splattering the windshield.

"The teeth are mine!" Purple Claw shrieked. "*Mine! Mine! Mine!*"

Then suddenly a black shadow fell over him, and the boat flew into the air.

Purple Claw frantically wrenched the steering wheel—left! right! left!—thinking he had been hit by a wave. But the boat kept rising.

He stood up and peered out over the windshield. Then he let out a terrible squeal.

He was caught in a fishing net!

"Help!" he cried as Arthur and Lucy gazed at him in astonishment. They thought he looked very odd.

And it wasn't just his long black cape or his scarlet boots or his purple claws that were so unusual. He was simply the mangiest, meanest, most horrible-looking mouse they had ever seen.

"Are Uncle Jeremy's teeth in there?" Lucy said, peering into the net.

"They must be in that candy tin," Arthur replied.

But Purple Claw looked so nasty, neither child dared to reach down a hand to take it out.

Tumtum and Nutmeg and Lord Seamouse watched in delight from behind the pebble.

"What will they do with him?" they all asked. The children were wondering just the same thing.

He didn't look like the sort of mouse one would wish to keep as a pet. And yet he was a villain, so now that they had caught him, they couldn't just let him go.

"Let's take him back to Smugglers' Keep and tip him out into the bathtub," Arthur suggested.

"All right," Lucy said. "Uncle Jeremy will know what to do with him. Now that we've found the treasure, we can tell him the whole story."

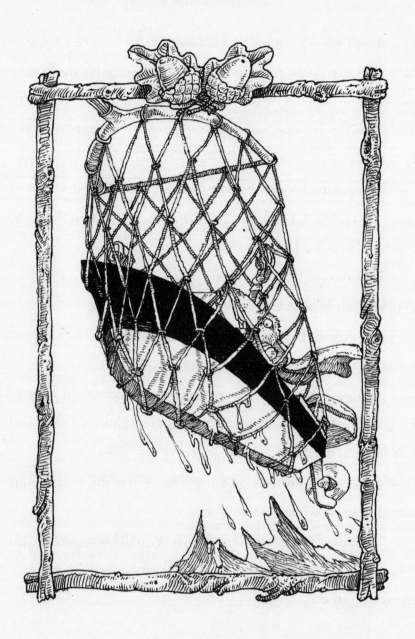

They hurried back across the beach.

Lucy carried the fishing net full of the dollhouse furniture, and Arthur carried the net containing Purple Claw, who squealed and scrabbled all the way home.

Tumtum and Nutmeg and Lord Seamouse followed them. But they couldn't run as fast as the children, so they trailed some way behind.

When the children got back to Smugglers' Keep, Mrs. Blythe let them in.

"What have you caught in there?" she asked Arthur, seeing the net swinging back and forth on the end of his rod.

"Er, nothing . . ." Arthur mumbled, edging past her.

The children didn't want Mrs. Blythe to see Purple Claw, or she would be sure to start shrieking again.

"Just something we fished out of the Rock Pool," Lucy explained hurriedly. Then they fled upstairs before she could ask any more questions.

They ran into the bathroom and locked themselves in. Then Arthur shook the fishing net over the bathtub, and Purple Claw and the boat and the candy tin all tipped out.

Purple Claw tore up and down, trying to escape. But the bathtub was very deep, and he couldn't get out.

He saw Arthur and Lucy peering down at him and shook his fists with rage.

"You hateful little creatures!" he cried. "I'll get my revenge for this! Just you wait and see!" But all the children heard was a squeal.

When Purple Claw was at the other end of the bathtub, Lucy quickly reached down and picked up the tin.

Purple Claw gave a howl and rushed toward her, gnashing his fangs.

But the bathtub was so slippery he skidded over and landed flat on his back, kicking his scarlet boots in the air.

Lucy pried off the lid of the tin, and the children looked inside. And there they were, Uncle Jeremy's milk teeth! It was very strange to see them.

"They must be ancient," Arthur said. "Nearly as old as he is!"

"We'd better give them back to him," Lucy said.

Arthur agreed, so they put the lid back on the tin, then

222

they left Purple Claw alone in the bathtub and went downstairs.

Uncle Jeremy was in the drawing room, reading a book about fishing. He could see from the children's faces that something very serious had taken place.

And when they showed him the tin of teeth, and told him that they all belonged to him, from when he was a little boy, he was very surprised.

He had given his teeth to the tooth fairies. He hadn't expected to see them again.

"Wherever did you find them?" he said.

So the children told him the whole story, beginning with the map on the bedside table and ending with Purple Claw's dramatic capture in the Rock Pool.

The only thing they left out was Nutmeg, for she had warned them ages ago that they must never tell anyone about her. But after she had left the map on the bedside table, she didn't come into the story much. So they managed not to mention her.

Uncle Jeremy listened very carefully. He didn't interrupt,

and he didn't make them feel silly, as some grown-ups might have done.

"So what did you do with Purple Claw?" he asked.

"He's upstairs in the bathtub!" Lucy said. "Come and have a look at him. He's the strangest mouse you've ever seen."

Uncle Jeremy didn't really believe that the children had found a mouse with purple claws, of course. But he didn't want to spoil their fun. So he levered himself out of his chair and followed them upstairs.

Lucy opened the bathroom door and let him go in first. And when he saw Purple Claw, he got such a fright that he fell over backward and crashed into the towel rail.

It was just as the children had said . . . an angry, mangy little mouse, with a black cape and scarlet boots . . . and *purple claws*!

Uncle Jeremy pulled off his spectacles and gave them a good polish. Then he stood up and peered into the bathtub again.

"Astonishing. Quite astonishing. Quite, quite astonishing," he said over and over again. He had seen mice before in Smugglers' Keep — but never one like this.

"What will we do with him?" the children asked.

"We must treat him like a king!" Uncle Jeremy replied. "Go down to the kitchen and ask Mrs. Blythe for the finest mouse-size morsels she can find. Bring him cheese and chocolates and the tastiest slivers of ham!"

"What's he done to deserve that?" Arthur asked.

"Don't you see? He is a rare breed!" cried Uncle Jeremy, hopping around the room in excitement. "He's the rarest of the rare! The strangest of the strange! We must put him in a cage and lend him to the zoo, so that everyone can come and look at him! He will be the most famous mouse in the whole wide world!"

## Chapter Sixteen

The rest of the day passed in a daze.

Uncle Jeremy telephoned all the local newspapers, and soon the house was full of reporters and photographers jostling to see Purple Claw in the bathtub.

Everyone wanted to ask the children questions:

"So this mouse who appeared on the dining room table was wearing a suit, you say?"

"And he left you a letter?"

"And he signed himself 'General Marchmouse'?"

Somehow, the children sensed that the reporters didn't believe a word they were saying.

"They think we've made it up," Arthur whispered, when he and Lucy finally had a moment on their own.

"But they've seen Purple Claw, so they must know it's true," Lucy said.

"They probably think we dressed him up in doll clothes and painted his toes purple ourselves," Arthur said. "You know what grown-ups are like."

It was true, grown-ups could be awful. The children started wishing they would all go away.

But then suddenly one of the reporters pointed across the room and let out a shriek.

The other reporters all turned to look. And to their astonishment, they saw a little mouse marching up and down the mantelpiece, swishing a match at them.

And he was dressed in a green suit!

"Don't believe a word those children tell you!" he roared. "*I* discovered the treasure first, and if it hadn't been for me, no one would ever have found it! It was all thanks to *me*! The great General Marchmouse!"

No one could understand a word he was saying, of course — for, to the human ear, his voice was just a squeal. But the Gen-

eral didn't care. He strutted up and down, boasting and saluting, and causing a terrible stir.

The reporters became very excited and started shouting into their cell phones, saying, "Hold the front page!"

Everyone was egging the General on.

The General was a natural show-off, and he didn't need much encouragement. He puffed his chest, and preened his whiskers, and posed beside a china shepherdess.

The children stood at the back of the room, watching with delight.

"They'll have to believe us now!" Arthur said.

The General showed off for a whole hour solid. Then one of the reporters cried, "Come on! Let's catch him, and take him back to the office in a cardboard box!"

"Just you try!" the General roared. Then he leaped to the floor and shot out the door, moving so fast no one could stop him.

Tumtum and Nutmeg and Lord Seamouse had just returned from the beach. As they came inside, they heard a terrible commotion.

They crept across the kitchen floor and peeked into the hall—just in time to see General Marchmouse fleeing from the drawing room.

"General, over here!" Tumtum cried.

The General shot toward them, then they all darted into the vegetable rack, and hid inside the leaves of a cabbage.

The reporters saw the General fleeing into the kitchen and stormed after him.

"He must be here somewhere!" they cried, and started going through the cupboards. The mice trembled in the cabbage, terrified they would search the vegetable rack, too. But when Mrs. Blythe saw what a mess the people were making, she shooed them away with a dishcloth.

Finally, the kitchen was quiet. But the mice were very shaken. "Whatever's been going on?" Nutmeg whispered.

"Some reporters came to see me," the General replied grandly. "They tried to kidnap me—I think they wanted to make me into a television star!"

"What a terrible thought!" Tumtum shuddered.

They could still hear people clonking around in the hall.

"Let's stay here until everyone's gone," Nutmeg said. "We don't want to take any more chances."

They stayed hidden inside the cabbage for a long time. They waited until the last reporter had left the house and until they had heard Uncle Jeremy and the children going upstairs to bed. Only when everything was absolutely quiet and still did they dare to clamber out of the vegetable rack and start creeping back to Seaview Hollow.

But as they were passing the drawing-room door, they heard someone snoring. And when they peeked inside, they saw the most astonishing sight. In the middle of the floor was a big cage, with a domed roof and gold bars. It was the most magnificent cage they had ever seen, almost like a palace.

They crept over to it and looked through the bars. And there was Purple Claw — and didn't he look grand! He was fast asleep in a bed of duck feathers, with a swollen stomach, and a dreamy smile on his face. Beside his bed was a pretty china trough, full of raisins and pastry crumbs, and chips and chocolates, and slivers of the finest, smelliest cheese.

"These bars look very flimsy. I wouldn't be surprised if he manages to break out!" Lord Seamouse said anxiously.

"Oh, he won't do that," Tumtum said. "Just see how fat and content he looks. He's the luckiest villain there ever was!"

Tumtum was quite right, of course. Purple Claw had done very well for himself—much better than he deserved. The next morning, he would be taken to the zoo, where he would live happily ever after in his gilded cage, being photographed and fussed over, and given delicious things to eat.

And he would never bother another mouse again.

Finally, the Nutmouses, the General, and Lord Seamouse clambered upstairs and crept into Arthur and Lucy's bedroom. The children were asleep, but the mice crossed the floor on tiptoe all the same. But when they saw the dollhouse, they all let out a cheer.

For it was a splendid sight. The children had put all the furniture back in place, and arranged all the tapestries and the paintings and the lamps and the candlesticks. They had even made Lord Seamouse's bed!

"Gracious," Tumtum said enviously. "It's even grander than Nutmouse Hall!"

When he saw all his pretty things again, Lord Seamouse shed a tear. His dark days in Seaview Hollow were over. Now he would be Lord Seamouse of Seaview Manor again!

"Come in, come in!" he said, longing to show the other mice around. He took them upstairs and downstairs, and everyone was very impressed.

"Oh, look!" Lord Seamouse cried when they came to the drawing room. For there were Uncle Jeremy's teeth, neatly arranged in the glass cabinet! How delightful to see them back on display!

And when they reached the dining room, they found that the children had left them a dish of breadcrumbs and a whole chunk of chocolate for their dinner.

Lord Seamouse sliced the chocolate with his carving knife and served everything on his best silver plates, then they all sat talking and eating late into the night.

And there we must leave them, for their adventures are over, at least for now. And Arthur's and Lucy's adventures are over, too. But there was so much chatter and laughter coming from the dollhouse that, as the night wore on, Lucy started to toss and turn. And it was a funny thing, but as she was drifting back to sleep, she could have sworn she saw someone peeking at her from the bedside table. Someone with a long, nutmeg tail.

# A Circus
# Adventure

## Chapter One

General Marchmouse swaggered past the compost heap with a song rising in his heart. He had a good reason to be cheerful. Today was his birthday! And mice do not have nearly as many birthdays as humans do, so it was a very special day indeed.

He had been busy since breakfast time, opening his cards and unwrapping his presents. And now it was almost dark, but the best part of the day was about to come. Tonight his friends Tumtum and Nutmeg had invited him for a birthday feast at Nutmouse Hall.

*Perhaps Nutmeg will have made a spider pie*, he thought hungrily. *And a toad-in-the-hole, and a cockroach soufflé, and a strawberry tart with toasted almonds on top!*

He hurried on under the rosebushes and clambered down onto the garden path with his invitation clutched tightly in his paw.

It was a cold November evening, and he was glad to see Rose Cottage looming ahead of him. The curtains were still open, and all the windows were brightly lit.

"Hmm. It looks like the Mildews are at home," the General muttered. "I shall have to be very careful—Tumtum will be furious if I give his hiding place away."

He crept up to the back door and cautiously peeked his nose into the kitchen. There was a spider dozing on the doormat and a cockroach scuttling beneath the sink. But there were no humans in sight, so he set off across the floor.

The General had visited Nutmouse Hall many times before, so he knew just where to go. It was a very grand house, built inside the Mildews' broom cupboard. And its front gates were hidden beneath the old wooden dresser that stood against the kitchen wall.

The General marched along, taking his usual route—past

the laundry basket, under the vegetable rack, then around the leg of the kitchen table.

He hadn't far to go, and when he peered under the dresser he could see a tiny beam of light coming from the Nutmouses' gates. He hurried on, wading through a puddle of ketchup on the floor.

But then suddenly he stepped into a dark shadow. And when he looked up, he saw the most amazing sight.

*It was a circus top!*

The General froze and stared at it in astonishment. It was the finest circus top he had ever seen. It had red and green stripes, and it was bigger than a beach ball. And standing beside it was a little ticket booth with velvet curtains.

The General felt his heart quicken. *It must be a mouse circus,* he thought, *for everything is mouse-sized! Well, whomever it belongs to is a very lucky mouse, that's for sure!*

He stood there a moment, gazing admiringly at the big top. He wondered if there were dancing dragonflies or racing slugs inside, or any of the other wonderful things that mouse circuses usually have.

241

He decided to go in and see. But when he reached the entrance, he saw a silver card lying on the ground with HAPPY BIRTHDAY! written on the front.

"Well, I never!" the General said. "This circus must be a present for me!"

The birthday card was bigger than he was. He hoisted it open, wondering who it was from. But when he read what it said, his face fell:

*Dear Arthur,*

   *This is a toy circus that I was given long ago, when I was not much older than you are now. I hope you enjoy playing with it as much as I did.*

   *Happy birthday!*

   *Love,*

   *Uncle Jeremy*

"Humph!" the General grunted. "It must be Arthur's birthday, too. So it's not a mouse circus after all — it's just a toy!"

The General thought it was very unfair that the circus was

242

given to Arthur instead of him. "It's far too good for a boy!" he said crossly.

He was still curious to see what was inside the big top. So he pulled open the flap and marched through. And how he stared! For he had entered an enormous stadium, with bleachers around the edges and a trapeze up above. And in front of him was a huge crowd of circus animals — wooden horses and leopards, and tigers and elephants, all parading around the ring.

The General rubbed his eyes in astonishment. The toys looked so real that for a moment he thought they were! And standing in their midst was a toy ringmaster, dressed in a shiny gold suit and holding a whip.

"Lucky fellow," the General muttered. How he wished that he had a gold suit, too! What fun it would be to stand in the middle of the ring, making the toy animals dance to the crack of his whip!

He stood there a long time, filled with envy. From somewhere in Rose Cottage, he heard the clock chime seven. He knew Tumtum and Nutmeg would be wondering where he was,

for he was late for dinner. And yet he couldn't tear himself away.

"Surely there can't be any harm in just trying the suit on and having one tiny crack of the whip," he reasoned. "It is my birthday, after all!"

He glanced guiltily over his shoulder. And after a very short period of hesitation, he marched up to the ringmaster and tore off his clothes. He tugged off his own Royal Mouse Army uniform and tossed it to the floor. Then he pulled on the gold pants. They were very tight, and he had to take a big breath in order to do up the button. But the jacket was a perfect fit.

He strutted around the ring, feeling very grand.

Then he snatched the whip and gave it a hard crack. "March!" he shouted. The lions shook, and an elephant toppled to the floor. The General whooped with joy — oh, what fun!

On he went, swaggering and shouting and cracking his whip, until soon all the wooden animals had been thrashed to the ground. No creature was spared. An elephant's trunk had snapped off, and one of the lions had lost a leg.

The General wondered what to do next.

Then he had a daring plan. *I know!* he thought. *I shall go and catch that cockroach I saw scuttling off under the sink, and train it to swing on the trapeze!*

He tucked the whip under his arm and ran out of the tent. But as he stepped into the kitchen, he got a terrible fright. Arthur and Lucy had appeared!

The General gulped and dived back inside the big top. He had been making such a racket that he hadn't heard them come downstairs. He knew he was in terrible trouble, for Arthur would be furious if he found him here and saw what he had done to his toys.

He stood trembling, listening to the children's feet thudding on the floor.

"Just look at my circus!" Arthur said proudly. "Isn't it the most splendid circus you've ever seen? I don't mind one bit that Pa forgot my birthday—this circus makes up for everything. Come on, let's play with it again."

"All right," Lucy replied. "Wait a second while I put the milk bottles out."

246

The General's mind whirled with terror. He heard Lucy open the garden door and clank the bottles outside. Then he saw the children's shadows looming over the tent. . . .There was nowhere he could hide. . . .

There was a rustle, then the flap of the tent slowly opened, and a huge pink hand reached inside. . . .

"Oh, what am I to do?" The General quivered. "It's my birthday, and I'm going to be caught!"

But the General was a very lucky mouse. At that very moment, as if by a miracle, the telephone rang.

"I bet that's Uncle Jeremy, calling to check that the circus has arrived!" Arthur said.

The children both jumped up and ran into the hall.

The General seized his chance to escape. In his haste, he forgot all about his army uniform and dashed out of the big top wearing the ringmaster's clothes. Then he turned and hurtled toward Nutmouse Hall.

But as he skirted around the big top, he saw something so completely and utterly dazzling that for a moment it made him forget all his fear. It was a bus. But not just any bus. This was, quite simply, the most splendid, most beautiful bus the General had *ever* seen.

It was gleaming red, with shining headlights and silver wheels the size of saucers. He crept up to it and pressed his nose to the window. There was a fat leather steering wheel and a gear-shift as big as a lollipop. And in the back of the bus were two little camp beds, with green quilts and crisp white pillows.

The General's whiskers twitched. The bus looked very inviting. He could hear Arthur and Lucy talking on the tele-phone in the hall. He knew they might come back into the kitchen at any moment, but he was too excited to care.

Then suddenly he felt a cold breeze cutting his ankles, and when he looked around he saw to his surprise that the children had left the garden door open.

He stood there for a moment, peering out. The sky had turned black, but he could see the pale outline of the garden path, twisting away in the moonlight.

And suddenly it was as if the moon and the stars were all calling out to him, whispering his name.

With a pounding heart, he pulled open the bus door and clambered into the driver's seat, tossing the whip beside him. Then he gripped the steering wheel and turned on the ignition.

The engine gave a shudder, then a *Vroom!*, and the bus shot forward across the floor.

"Faster! Faster!" the General cried, slamming his paw on the accelerator. He swerved under the kitchen table and tore toward the open door.

The spider fled out of his way, and a fly splattered on the windshield. The General clung tightly to his seat as the bus bounced over the doorstep and crashed onto the garden path. Then, with a shriek of joy, he turned on his headlights and sped into the night.

# Chapter Two

Nutmeg had been bustling and baking all afternoon, preparing the General's birthday feast. While she worked, Tumtum dozed in the library. When everything was nearly ready, he woke up and wandered into the kitchen, hoping to find a spoon to lick.

"Isn't it a coincidence that Arthur and the General have a birthday on the very same day?" he said, dipping his paw into one of Nutmeg's mixing bowls.

"Yes, isn't it!" Nutmeg agreed. "Oh, Tumtum, wouldn't it be lovely if Arthur could come to the birthday feast, too? For you can be quite sure there won't be any feasting going on in Rose Cottage. I peeked out into the kitchen earlier this afternoon, and there was no sign of a cake!"

"Are the children having something special for dinner?" Tumtum asked.

"I don't think so," Nutmeg replied sadly. "When I last looked in their pantry, there was nothing except a stale loaf of bread and a few cans of spaghetti!"

Tumtum wrinkled his nose. He had tried canned spaghetti once, and he had not liked it at all. It was a great mystery to him how humans could bear to eat it.

"Yes, it's a pity the children are too big to fit through our mouse hole," he agreed. "Just think how astonished they would be if they could see all the delicious things *we* have to eat!"

"Well, at least Arthur got a nice birthday present," Nutmeg said, briskly rolling her pastry.

"Did he?" Tumtum asked in surprise. "Was it from his father?"

"Oh, gracious no! You know Mr. Mildew never remembers about presents!" Nutmeg said. "It was from his uncle Jeremy — you remember, the nice old man we all went to stay with last summer at the seaside. He sent Arthur a beautiful toy circus. I saw it when I went out this afternoon. Arthur's thrilled with it!

I heard him telling Lucy that it was the best present he'd ever had!"

"Oh, I am glad," Tumtum said, looking very relieved. It would have spoiled his appetite to think of Arthur having no presents as well as no cake. Now he could enjoy tonight's feast all the more.

"Now let's see," Nutmeg said, rubbing her paws on her apron. "I've still got to toast the croutons for the soup, and ice the cake, and glaze the ham, and chill the jellies, and warm the cockroach pastries. . . . Then I think we're all done!"

"Goodness, what a lot of food we have," Tumtum said. "It's enough to feed a hundred mice! But there will only be three of us, now that Mrs. Marchmouse can't come."

"Yes, it is a rotten shame that she can't be here." Nutmeg sighed. "But it's good of her to go and look after her sister. Apparently she's been very ill. Mrs. Marchmouse will probably have to stay with her for some time."

"Well, I shouldn't think the General will mind being left on his own," Tumtum said. "You know what he's like. He loves getting into trouble, but it's not so easy when Mrs. Marchmouse is watching over him!"

They both smiled. Mrs. Marchmouse had been keeping a very strict eye on the General lately. He would probably consider a few days on his own a nice birthday treat!

"Well, I shall make jolly sure that he doesn't get into trouble when he comes here," Nutmeg said firmly. "I'm not having him dragging us into another adventure."

"Certainly not," Tumtum agreed. "We've had quite enough of those! But you needn't worry, dear. The General will be much too busy eating to get into any of his silly games. The only trouble he's likely to encounter tonight is indigestion!"

Nutmeg laughed. And as she put the finishing touches on all her little dishes, she felt full of warm feelings. Tumtum was right; there would be no adventures tonight. Just lots of fun and hearty eating!

"Gracious!" Nutmeg exclaimed, looking at the clock. "He'll be here soon, and we still haven't set the table!"

They both hurried through to the dining room and lit all the candles. Then they set the table with their best silver and china, for today was a very special occasion.

When everything was ready, they went upstairs to change.

Nutmeg put on her pink dress, and Tumtum wore his velvet jacket. Then they settled down in the library and waited for the General to arrive.

But the time ticked by, and the clock struck seven — and still he did not appear.

"I hope he hasn't gotten lost," Nutmeg fussed.

"Oh, no, he knows the way much too well for that," Tumtum said. "He's probably just stopped to chase a beetle. You know what he's like!"

But Nutmeg still felt anxious, for it was unlike the General to be late for a meal.

They sat there a little longer, nervously sipping their cider. Then suddenly they heard raised voices coming from the Mildews' kitchen. It was Arthur and Lucy, and they sounded very upset.

Tumtum and Nutmeg could hear everything that was being said:

"But where is it? It can't just have disappeared!" Arthur cried.

"Well, I haven't taken it," Lucy said.

"Well, you must have. No one else has been in here today!" Arthur shouted.

"No, I haven't!" Lucy said angrily. "Why would I want to take your silly circus bus? I tell you, I haven't touched it."

"But you *must* have taken it," Arthur wailed. "I left it here, by the big top. It can't just have vanished into thin air!"

Tumtum and Nutmeg looked at each other in surprise. They knew all the comings and goings at Rose Cottage, and no one else had been there today.

"Arthur must be mistaken—no one could have taken the bus," Nutmeg said. "It was certainly there when I went out earlier, and I know no one's been in the kitchen since then...except—"

The mice looked at each other and gulped, for the same thought had entered both of their minds.

"Oh, Tumtum," Nutmeg whispered. "You don't think...I mean...you don't really think...Oh, *surely* the General couldn't have been wicked enough to steal Arthur's bus!"

# Chapter Three

Tumtum and Nutmeg hurried out of Nutmouse Hall and tiptoed to the edge of the dresser. They could see Arthur kneeling on the floor, his head lowered as he peered into the big top.

"Someone's knocked over all the animals," he cried. "And look—they've broken my wooden elephant *and* one of the lions!"

He turned around and glared at his sister. "It must have been you!" he shouted, holding up the broken toys for her to see. "Who else could have done it?"

"Oh, don't be so awful!" Lucy said. "I told you, I didn't touch your circus. I haven't been near it all day!"

Arthur scowled, but he knew Lucy was telling the truth. She wouldn't have broken his toys; she wasn't that sort of sister.

"Let me look inside," Lucy said, for she could see that he was very upset. Arthur shuffled aside, then Lucy knelt down in front of the big top and peeked in. And she noticed something very strange. "Look!" she said. "Someone's taken the ringmaster's clothes!" She reached in through the flap and pulled the toy out of the tent. And when Arthur saw it, he was amazed. When he had last played with it, it had been wearing a gold suit. But while he had been gone, someone had stripped it to its underpants!

"Hang on, here are some other clothes!" Lucy exclaimed, spotting the tiny garments that the General had tossed to the floor. She took them out and spread them on the palm of her hand. The children looked at them curiously.

"Look at these tiny gold medals on the jacket!" Arthur said. "It looks like an army uniform. But it's not like the uniform a toy soldier would have. It seems too . . . well . . . *too real!*"

Lucy agreed. "And isn't this strange?" she said, pointing to the jacket. "There are hairs on the collar! This can't belong to a toy. It must belong to something real.

"Whoever he is, he must have crept in here when we

weren't looking, then changed into the ringmaster's clothes and driven away in the bus!"

It was very mysterious, and the children were longing to find out who the secretive creature could be.

"Come on, let's find him!" Arthur said, running to grab the flashlight from the shelf by the back door. "The bus was still here when the telephone rang, so he can't have gotten far!"

Tumtum and Nutmeg were still crouched under the dresser. They watched in dismay as the children raced outside.

"So it *was* him!" Nutmeg said. "And to think that he even stole the ringmaster's clothes! Oh, Tumtum! How could he be so silly? And now the children are sure to catch him and lock him up in a cage!"

"It serves him right if they do," Tumtum said crossly. "Really, what a fool he's been!"

"But just think how upset Mrs. Marchmouse will be when she comes home and we have to tell her the General's been taken prisoner," Nutmeg said anxiously. "You remember how upset she was when it happened before!"

The children had once caught the General playing in their

dollhouse, and they had taken him to school with them and put him in a cage full of pet gerbils. Mrs. Marchmouse had been quite distraught.

Tumtum sighed. Nutmeg was right. It would be too awful if Mrs. Marchmouse had to go through that again.

"Let's see what's going on outside," he said. They crept over to the back door and peered anxiously into the garden.

The children were rushing back and forth, shining the flashlight around the lawn and the flower beds.

"Come on! It must be here somewhere," Arthur cried.

They searched high and low — around the vegetable patch, and the trash cans, and the compost heap — but the bus wasn't there.

"I don't understand it!" Arthur groaned. "It can't just have vanished!"

"We'll have to come and look again in the morning," Lucy said. "It's too dark now."

"All right," Arthur agreed, for they had been outside for ages, and his hands were turning numb with cold. "But I can tell you, whoever the thief is, he'll be sorry when I catch him!"

Tumtum and Nutmeg crouched behind the shoehorn

262

while Arthur and Lucy walked back inside. They did not speak until the children had gone upstairs.

"Well, I'm glad they didn't catch him—Arthur sounded very cross!" Nutmeg said. "But where can he be? They've looked everywhere!"

"He must have gone farther away," Tumtum said. "I'll bet he's driven down into the meadow! You know how much he loves to go exploring there, and just think how much fun he could have in a bus!"

"Oh, dear. You're probably right," Nutmeg said anxiously. She hadn't thought of the meadow. It was below Rose Cottage, and it was a wild place. It had a stream running along the bottom, and at night it was full of foxes. Tumtum was right; the General loved to go adventuring there. "I hope he doesn't come to any harm," she said.

"Oh, he'll be all right inside his bus," Tumtum said. "And you can be quite sure he'll turn up as soon as he's hungry. He won't want to miss his birthday feast! Now come on, we'd better get home in case the children come downstairs again."

They hurried across the kitchen and let themselves back into Nutmouse Hall. They were no longer in the mood for cider, so Nutmeg made a pot of tea, and they sat by the fire waiting for the General's familiar *Rap! Tap! Tap!* at the door.

But the hours slipped by, and when ten o'clock struck, he still hadn't appeared.

Nutmeg was very nervous.

"I wouldn't worry, dear; he's probably just decided to camp out for the night," Tumtum said, trying to raise her spirits. "You know how he can't resist an adventure. We might as well get some sleep. Then we can set out and look for him first thing in the morning."

Nutmeg agreed, for after her long day of baking and worrying, she felt very tired. And the house felt sad now that their party had been spoiled. So they blew out the candles in the dining room and climbed upstairs to bed.

But if they could only have seen what their friend was up to, they would not have slept a wink that night. For the General had fallen into a much bigger adventure than he had planned.

# Chapter Four

The General drove so fast, it was no wonder the children hadn't been able to find him. After leaving the cottage, he had sped straight to the far end of the garden, then slipped underneath the tall farm gate and into the meadow.

He heard an owl hoot and a fox howl, but he felt not a drop of fear. The night was his, and his whole body ached for adventure.

The General knew just where he wanted to go. He would drive all the way to the bottom of the meadow, and spend the night camping by the stream! The grass was taller than the hood of his bus, and the ground was rough. But he pressed on the accelerator and bumped along as fast as he could, plotting his adventure.

Tonight he would ambush a snoozing snail and roast it for his dinner. And tomorrow morning he would catch a beetle and make it trot around in circles to the crack of his whip. Then he'd put up a sign reading GENERAL MARCHMOUSE'S CIRCUS TROUPE, and invite all the field mice to his first show!

In his mind's eye, he saw himself strutting about in his gold suit, showing off to the crowd, and he felt a lovely warm glow in his stomach.

What a glorious adventure it promised to be! But adventures cannot be planned, as the General was about to discover.

For just as he was coming within sight of the stream, he saw something that surprised him. A little way off along the bank, there was a cluster of bright lights! On spotting them, he quickly stopped and turned off his engine, wondering what they could be.

At first he could not see much, for the moon had been swallowed by a cloud. But a few moments later, the cloud shifted in the breeze, and a pale moonlight dribbled along the bank. The General sat back in his seat with a jolt. For he could see now where the lights were coming from, and he could hardly believe it.

For lo and behold if it wasn't another circus — with wooden wagons and a big top! But this circus was no toy. It was a *real live* mouse circus — there could be no mistake of that. There was a snail roasting on a campfire, and the General could see four mice silhouetted against the tent.

He was *furious*. He couldn't set up his own circus now, this one would steal all his business! There hadn't been a mouse circus visiting the village for ages. It was just his luck that one should show up now.

"I can't let them spoil my adventure. I shall go and tell them to go away!" he decided. He grabbed his whip and slid out of the bus. Then off he marched toward the big top, grinding his teeth.

The circus was surrounded by a low fence lit with lanterns. And at the entrance there was a wooden booth with a sign reading TICKETS. The General knocked on the window, but there was no reply. He knocked again. Then he barged through the gate.

He looked around in surprise, for the circus did not look nearly as impressive from the inside. The ground was strewn with garbage, and the big top was full of holes.

268

The circus mice were sitting around their campfire, eating roasted flies. When they saw the General, they all looked up and snarled.

The General was taken aback, for the mice looked very sinister.

There were four of them, and they all had fiery red fur and piercing black eyes. One was as thin as a pipe cleaner and had a scar on his nose. He was dressed in a scarlet suit, and was clearly the ringmaster. The other three were dressed as clowns, but somehow they did not look at all like clowns should. Their mouths turned down at the corners, and their teeth were dark yellow.

"What are you doing here?" the ringmaster snarled.

"I've come to tell you to go away!" the General replied rudely. "There is only room for one circus in this meadow and..."

But before he could get any further, one of the clowns walked up and gave him a shove. "Who do you think you are, telling us to go away?" he shouted. "*You* go away! Go on, *SHOO!*"

The others had gathered behind him, looking at the General with menace. But the General was too angry to feel afraid.

"How dare you! Do you know who I am?" he raged. "I am the Great General Marchmouse, and I warn you now, if you mess with me, you will have the Royal Mouse Army to answer to!"

His words had a powerful effect. General Marchmouse was a very famous name in the mouse community, and the circus mice were clearly impressed.

The ringmaster gave a cold smile. And when he spoke, his voice sounded quite different. It was almost oily.

"General Marchmouse! This is an honor, to be sure! You will surely stay and share our roasted flies?"

The General was flustered by the ringmaster's sudden change in tone. It struck him that his voice sounded suspicious. But the flies did smell very delicious, and it seemed ages since he had last eaten.

"Well, all right then, I suppose I might have time for a quick bite," he said, eyeing the frying pan greedily.

One of the clowns handed him a plate, and they all sat down around the campfire. Once he had started munching his fly, the General felt quite chatty.

"Tell me, are you new to these parts?" he asked. "It's been ages since we last had a circus in the meadow."

"We just arrived here this afternoon," one of the clowns replied. "And we're doing our first show tomorrow. All the field mice are coming. We're nearly sold out."

"Gracious!" the General said. "And where are you all from?"

"Oh, we're town mice!" the ringmaster replied proudly. "I used to belong to the Red Top Circus, but I left a few months ago to set up on my own."

The General looked at him in amazement. "The Red . . . Y-you mean to say . . . *Good grief!*"

The General was very impressed. For the Red Top Circus was the most popular circus in the whole land. Mice traveled for miles to see its giant beetles and its dancing dragonflies and its racing slugs. As a schoolmouse, the General had saved his pocket money to see its shows, and had known the names of all the performers.

"By Jove!" he said.

The ringmaster looked very pleased. "Mr. Goldtail's my

name," he said, "and these are my clowns—Mr. Merry, Mr. Mirth, and Mr. Moody."

Everyone shook paws. "Goldtail, *Goldtail*..." the General said, racking his brains.

"Yes, yes...I'm sure I remember your name!" he said uncertainly. "Were you one of the trapeze mice, who shot out of a cannon?"

"That's right," Mr. Goldtail said quickly. "I was one of the best trapeze mice they'd ever had. But I wanted to be a ringmaster, so I left Red Top and set up on my own!"

"Good for you," the General said admiringly. He had been very upset to find another circus in the meadow, but he felt quite differently now that he knew whose circus it was.

"I must buy a ticket to your show," he said, digging in his pocket. But then his face fell. "Oh, drat," he muttered. "My wallet's in my jacket pocket—and I left my jacket in Arthur's big top!"

"Arthur's big top?" Mr. Goldtail asked anxiously. "But I haven't heard of Arthur's Circus. I thought *we* were the only mouse circus in these parts."

274

"Oh, Arthur's circus isn't a mouse circus!" the General laughed. And then he told them the whole story of his adventure so far — about how he had stumbled across a toy circus at Rose Cottage, and stolen the ringmaster's gold suit, and sped off in the shiny red bus before anyone could catch him.

Mr. Goldtail and his clowns laughed admiringly. They thought his story was very funny. No one showed any disapproval.

"There's my bus, over there," the General said proudly, pointing through the grass. "She's as fast as a hare — and she's got a horn and camp beds and real leather seats!"

The others all turned to look. And when they saw the big red bus gleaming in the moonlight, their jaws dropped in surprise.

No one said a word. The General could see they were very envious.

"Where's your bus?" he asked, feeling rather superior.

"We don't have one," Mr. Goldtail replied. "We had a squirrel to tow our wagons, but she escaped when we were unloading this morning, and now she's disappeared up one of these trees. It's a wretched nuisance. We want to move on after tomorrow's show, but we won't be able to go anywhere until we've caught another squirrel, and that could take weeks!"

The General pondered this. Then, because he was feeling starstruck, he made a rather careless suggestion.

"I say," he said. "Why don't you borrow my bus? I'm sure Arthur wouldn't mind if you took it for a day or two — and in return you can give me a ticket for tomorrow's show!"

The mice all looked very pleased.

"That's most kind of you," Mr. Goldtail said, his eyes glinting greedily.

Then he made a suggestion, too. "Why don't you join our circus?" he said. "You would make a fine beetle tamer, dressed in that splendid gold suit. And the crowds would come from far and wide if they heard that General Marchmouse was in the ring!"

"Oh, yes, what a smashing idea!" cried Mr. Mirth. "You could be our star attraction!"

The General looked overwhelmed. It was such a thrilling proposal, his brain had started to spin.

"It's a fine life in the circus," Mr. Merry said temptingly. "We'll give you your own wagon, with a dressing table, and chocolate truffles to eat!"

The General's heart quickened. He adored chocolate truffles.

"And you get lots of money!" purred Mr. Moody.

"And lots of fan mail!" Mr. Mirth added silkily.

Suddenly, all the mice were talking at once, egging him on. Their voices swam around him as if in a dream. The General closed his eyes and saw it all.... The crowds and the chocolates and the fan mail — and, above all, the open road, paved with adventure.

"Oh, yes!" he said. "I'LL COME!"

# Chapter Five

Nutmeg woke up first the next day. She sat up in bed and pulled her shawl around her. It was cold and bright. The sun was shining through the broom cupboard window, and she could hear a bird rustling in the bushes.

She turned to Tumtum and gave him a shake. "Wake up, dear!" she said. "It's time to go and find the General!"

Tumtum groaned, and buried his head under the covers. He didn't like waking up.

Nutmeg left him in bed and hurried downstairs to the kitchen. A little while later, Tumtum smelled sausages cooking.

*Perhaps I will get up after all*, he thought.

He got dressed, and soon he and Nutmeg were having a big breakfast in the kitchen. After the sausages there were oatmeal and pancakes and eggs, then a fruit salad with cherries on top. And they washed it all down with milk and hot coffee.

Tumtum felt much more cheerful once his stomach was full. "Well, we'd better be setting off," he said, wiping the crumbs from his whiskers.

It was still early when they crept out into the kitchen of Rose Cottage, and no one had stirred. The toy circus towered before them, with the big top flapping in the draft.

"If we find the General quickly, then we can have the bus back in place by the time the children come down for breakfast," Nutmeg said. "Just think how pleased they'll be to get it back!"

"Hmm, it should be possible," Tumtum said. "It's a Saturday, so the children will probably get up late. Come on, let's hurry up and find him. He can't have gone far in a small bus like that."

They ran across the kitchen and wriggled outside under the garden door. Then they crossed the path and scrambled onto the lawn. They were glad they had put on their rain boots, for the grass came up to their waists, and it was soaked with dew.

They were in little doubt as to which way the General had gone. They trekked straight down to the farm gate at the bottom of the garden and hurried into the meadow.

"Look how tall this gate is," Nutmeg said, peering up at it. "The bottom bar's so high up off the ground, there would have been plenty of room for the bus to go underneath."

They walked on, but soon the grass became taller than their heads, and they couldn't see where they were going. It was like being in a forest.

"Oh, dear. We'll never be able to find the bus now!" Nutmeg said anxiously.

But then Tumtum saw a big rock poking out of the grass just ahead of them. "Let's climb up on that. Then we'll be able to see where we are," he said.

They traipsed over to it and scrambled to the top. And when they stood up, they could see the whole meadow sloping away in front of them. Tumtum perched his field glasses on his nose and carefully scanned all over the meadow.

"Can you see anything?" Nutmeg asked impatiently.

"There he is!" Tumtum cried finally. "There's something

red down by the stream! I can't see it clearly; it's too far away. But it must be him!"

He passed Nutmeg the field glasses, so she could have a look, too. "Yes, that must be the bus," she said, seeing something red and shiny through the lenses. "But what's that big thing next to it? It looks like a balloon—or a huge tent. How very strange!"

Tumtum looked again, and now he saw it, too. Nutmeg was right; it did look like a tent. But it was too far off for him to be sure. "How very odd," he said. "Come on, let's go and investigate."

They scrambled down from the rock and started making their way through the grass. It was a long way, and it was nearly two hours later before they reached the other side of the meadow.

The grass around the stream was much shorter, and they could see all the way along the bank. And when they spotted Mr. Goldtail's big top, with Arthur's bus drawn up beside it, they stopped still in surprise.

"It must be a touring mouse circus!" Nutmeg said. "But I didn't know there was a circus coming to the meadow.

How strange that they didn't put up posters around the village!"

"Hmm. And it looks like the General's gotten mixed up with them somehow," Tumtum said anxiously. "Come on, we'd better go and see what's going on."

They hurried toward the gate. And when they reached the ticket booth, they found a notice pinned to the window:

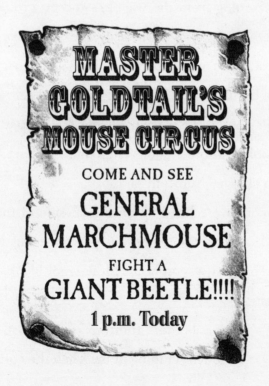

MASTER GOLDTAIL'S MOUSE CIRCUS

COME AND SEE

GENERAL MARCHMOUSE

FIGHT A

GIANT BEETLE!!!!

1 p.m. Today

"He's joined the circus!" Nutmeg gasped.

"Well, he'll un-join it soon enough when I've spoken to him!" Tumtum said crossly. "What nonsense! I'll soon talk some sense into him!"

He peered in the window of the ticket booth. There was no one inside, so they walked in through the gate.

The circus seemed deserted; there was no one in sight and not a sound coming from the wagons. And everything looked very shabby. Nutmeg was surprised. She had been taken to mouse circuses as a child, but they had all been spick-and-span—not a bit like this.

Something about the place made her feel uneasy.

"Let's look in those wagons over there and see if we can find who's in charge," Tumtum said.

The wagons were lined up on the far side of the big top. They walked over to them nervously, wondering what they would find. The first wagon had a filthy wool blanket hanging across the bars.

"I say, is anyone at home?" Tumtum asked.

There was a sudden scraping noise. Then the corner of the

blanket moved aside — and a big beetle glared out. When he saw Tumtum and Nutmeg, he gave an angry hiss. He did not look at all pleased to be disturbed.

They hastily apologized and tried the next wagon. But this one was just full of cardboard boxes, sealed with brown tape and labeled FRAGILE.

"I wonder what's in them," Nutmeg said curiously.

"Oh, probably just some circus junk," Tumtum said. He wasn't interested in the boxes. He just wanted to find the General and go home.

The third wagon had a plush red curtain drawn across it and a sign reading DO NOT DISTURB.

"Perhaps this is the ringmaster's wagon," Tumtum said. "It says not to disturb him, but I'm afraid we shall have to!"

Nutmeg watched anxiously as Tumtum stepped forward and called out through the curtain.

"I say, sorry to disturb you, but it's Mr. and Mrs. Nutmouse here, from Nutmouse Hall and — er, well . . . we just wondered if we could have a quick word with you, if you would be so kind. You see, we're looking for our friend. . . ."

There was no reply, and they wondered if the wagon might be empty.

But then they heard someone yawn. It was a long, bored yawn. The sort of yawn that says, "Oh, go away and leave me alone!"

The next moment, the curtain swished aside, and General Marchmouse appeared!

The Nutmouses looked at him in astonishment. This was not the General Marchmouse of yesterday, or the day before that. He had *completely* changed.

He was dressed in the gold suit that he had stolen from Arthur's ringmaster, and he had a daisy in his buttonhole — and his whiskers had been dyed bright pink! He did not look at all as a General should.

"Darlings, hello," he purred, in a voice most unlike his usual one. "Have you come to see the show?"

"Certainly not!" sputtered Tumtum, who found the General's new style most unsettling. "What are you playing at, General? How *dare* you steal Arthur's bus? You must drive us all back to Rose Cottage at once and return it to the kitchen!"

"I'm afraid that is out of the question," the General replied, peering down at them snootily. "I have lent the bus to Mr. Goldtail, seeing as he has no transportation of his own. And we shall need it this afternoon, when we drive off on the next stage of our tour!"

Tumtum and Nutmeg looked at him in horror. "*A TOUR!* Don't be so ridiculous!" Tumtum said. "Just think what Mrs. Marchmouse would say if she discovered you were touring with a circus! You are coming home with us!"

The General gave Tumtum a withering stare. His eyes had a stubborn gleam. "Oh, no, I am not!" he said tauntingly. "Can't you see, old boy? I'm a circus mouse now!"

## Chapter Six

Tumtum and Nutmeg did all they could to make the General be reasonable.

"Just think what the *Mouse Times* will say when they learn that the Great General Marchmouse has joined a circus!" Tumtum cried. "You'll be a laughingstock! The Royal Mouse Army will disown you!"

Tumtum felt sure this would bring the General to his senses, for he took great pride in his army career. But the General didn't seem to care.

"It's no good. I'm not coming," he said stubbornly. "My army days are over. I've become a star of the circus, and I shall become the biggest star there ever was! Now leave me alone. I've got to curl my whiskers for the show!"

And with that he stood up and swished shut the curtains.

Tumtum and Nutmeg were aghast.

"How *could* he be so beastly?" Nutmeg cried. "Can you imagine what Mrs. Marchmouse will say when we tell her he's run away to become a beetle tamer? Oh, if only we hadn't invited him to dinner at Nutmouse Hall, then none of this would have happened!"

"I've an idea," Tumtum whispered. "Let's drive the bus back to Rose Cottage ourselves! We've every right to take it — it belongs to Arthur, after all. And without a bus, the circus can't drive away. They'll be stuck here in the meadow until they find another means of transportation. So in the meantime at least we shall know where the General is."

"Oh, what a splendid idea!" Nutmeg said. "We can let the General have his fun until Mrs. Marchmouse comes home. Then *she* can come down here and talk some sense into him."

Feeling very cheered by this plan, they slipped away from the General's wagon and crept over to the bus.

But when Tumtum tried the driver's door, it was locked. And the passenger door was locked, too.

"Oh no!" he said.

"Let's see if the back door's open," Nutmeg suggested—but then there was a sudden shout.

"Hey! What are you doing?" a furious voice cried. "Get away from that bus!"

They both jumped. And when they turned around, they saw a clown marching toward them. It was Mr. Merry. His teeth were bared, and he looked very frightening.

"I, er...We were just, um...just admiring it," she said nervously.

"Well, now that you've admired it, you can leave," the clown replied.

"That's no way to speak to—"Tumtum began, but then Nutmeg gave him a sharp nudge. She sensed it was time to go.

"Shh," she whispered, "don't get into a fight." She tugged Tumtum by the sleeve, and they hurried out through the gate while the clown stood glaring at them.

"Let's get away," Nutmeg whispered. They walked on along the bank, until the circus was out of sight. Then they sat down on a rock, feeling very shaken.

"Isn't it strange that a clown should be so awful?" Nutmeg said. "In fact, there's something strange about the whole circus. I didn't see any dragonflies or racing slugs, or the sort of things that a mouse circus usually has. There was just one tired old beetle. And their big top was in tatters, but the General's wagon had a fancy chandelier. And did you notice those silver plates on his dressing table? I wonder where they got them from."

"Hmm, it did seem odd," Tumtum agreed. "I'd like to go back and have another snoop. But I don't want to run into that clown again. I reckon we've already made him suspicious. There's no point asking him for the bus back—I shouldn't think he'd care one bit if we told him it really belongs to Arthur!"

Nutmeg agreed. "But we *must* get it back before this afternoon," she said, "or else the circus will drive away, taking the General with them! You can see that he's completely under their spell! And just think what a fool he's going to look if word of this gets out. His reputation as a famous war hero will be ruined!"

The situation did look bleak. They both sat on the rock, wondering what to do.

Then Tumtum had an idea. "I know!" he said, jumping up

excitedly. "Let's go home and write the children a letter, telling them that their bus has been stolen by another circus. We can explain exactly where it is—they know the stream very well. Then they can come down here this afternoon and fetch it back!"

"Oh, what an excellent plan!" Nutmeg agreed.

But then she looked worried. "What about the General?" she said anxiously. "I mean, if the children find him sitting there curling his whiskers in his wagon, they might take him prisoner!"

"Oh, I wouldn't worry," Tumtum said. "The children are so big, the General and the circus mice will spot them from a mile away, and they'll hide in the grass. And without a bus, the circus won't seem nearly so appealing to the General. He'll give up the whole thing and head for home before anyone finds out about his silly adventure!"

"Oh, I do hope so," Nutmeg said.

There was no time to lose, so they hurried straight back across the meadow. But it took even longer this time, for they were going uphill. It was nearly midday by the time they reached the farm gate leading into the garden of Rose Cottage.

"At last!" Tumtum said, and at the sight of home his

294

stomach gave a loud rumble. It seemed ages since breakfast, and he could hardly wait to have a nice big lunch in his cozy kitchen.

But as they were walking under the gate, a field mouse appeared. The Nutmouses recognized him at once. It was little Timmy Twigmouse, whose father delivered the firewood to Nutmouse Hall. He appeared to be in a great hurry, and he looked very excited.

"Have you heard the news?" he asked breathlessly. "There's a circus in the meadow, and would you believe it? . . . *General Marchmouse has joined them!*"

Tumtum and Nutmeg gulped. News of the General's adventure had spread faster than they'd thought.

"When did you hear about this?" Tumtum asked anxiously.

"Oh, everyone's talking about it," Timmy Twigmouse squeaked. "The General's the star act. He's going to FIGHT A GIANT BEETLE! Just think! It's going to be quite a show!

"I say!" he said, noticing that they did not look very enthusiastic. "You are going, aren't you?"

"Oh, I don't think we have time today," Tumtum said vaguely, not wishing to reveal what they knew. "We'll go tomorrow."

"But you can't go tomorrow!" Timmy Twigmouse cried. "They won't be here tomorrow. Haven't you heard? This is a *ONE TIME SHOW*! And when it's finished they're packing up and moving on to London. Their next performance will be in Covent Garden!"

Tumtum and Nutmeg looked at him in horror.

"London!" Nutmeg gasped. "Are you sure?"

Timmy Twigmouse nodded. "That's right," he said. "My father went over this morning to deliver them some firewood, and they told him all about it. They're going to drive all the way there in their new circus bus! This is the only chance to see them, so I'm going down there right now to make sure I get tickets!"

Timmy Twigmouse said goodbye and hurried on his way. But Tumtum and Nutmeg stood by the gate, frozen with shock. They had never been to London, but they had heard all sorts of horrible things about it.

"*London!*" Nutmeg said faintly. "But London's miles away! And the mice there are all bandits! Oh, Tumtum, we *must* stop him! Just think what kind of trouble he might get into there!"

# Chapter Seven

After Tumtum and Nutmeg left, the General sat down at his dressing table, feeling a little deflated. Tumtum's words kept echoing around his head: "Think what Mrs. Marchmouse will say....Think what the *Mouse Times* will say....You will be a disgrace...disgrace...disgrace..."

The General pressed his paws over his ears, trying to block the voice out. "*Forget Tumtum!*" he muttered. "This is too good an adventure to miss. I'm not going to let him spoil my fun!"

He glanced in the mirror, thinking he would cheer up when he saw how handsome he looked. But even his reflection had lost its dazzle.

He stood up with a sigh and took his whip from the bed.

He was sure he would feel all right again once the show had begun.

"Tumtum is quite wrong, a beetle tamer is a very fine thing to be!" he told himself firmly. "When Mrs. Marchmouse hears about it, she'll be proud of me! And she isn't due back from her sister's until Friday. . . . Our tour will probably have finished by then, and I shall be back home, so it's not as though she'll miss me!"

He felt a little happier. And he decided to go and find Mr. Goldtail to discuss his act. The show was due to start in less than two hours, but there had been no dress rehearsal.

But just as he was opening the door of his wagon, Mr. Mirth appeared. He looked very agitated.

"Quick! Get in the bus! We're moving on!" he shouted.

"Moving on? But I don't understand," the General said in astonishment. "What about the show? The fans will be arriving soon."

"Just do what I say — and hurry!" Mr. Mirth snapped. Then he ran on down the line of wagons, slamming the doors, and fastening the towropes.

When the General stepped outside, he saw that all the other mice were rushing about, too. Mr. Moody was pouring water on the campfire, and Mr. Merry and Mr. Goldtail were pulling down the big top!

The General could not understand it. "What's happening?" he asked. But everyone was too frantic to explain.

In almost no time, the big top and the ticket booth had been loaded onto the wagons.

"Right, that's everything!" Mr. Goldtail shouted, leaping behind the wheel of the bus. "Come on, everyone. Jump in, QUICK!"

The clowns all leaped on board. Only the General remained on the ground.

"*COME ON!*" Mr. Goldtail shouted, poking his head through the window. "Hurry, or we'll be caught!"

"*Caught?* Caught by whom?" the General asked—but then suddenly he heard a piercing whistle, so loud it made him jump.

Mr. Goldtail revved the engine, and the bus and the wagons lurched forward through the grass. The General did not know

where the whistle was coming from, or whose whistle it was. But he felt sure that something awful was going to happen.

"Wait for me!" he cried, running after them. Mr. Mirth opened the back door and hauled him inside. Then off they sped along the bank, with the six wooden wagons clattering behind them.

Mr. Goldtail drove the bus as fast as it would go. *Bump, bump, bump* they went until they reached the edge of the field. Then they scraped through the bushes and into the woods on the other side.

The clowns kept looking anxiously through the back windshield to see if they were being followed. The mood was very tense. No one said a word.

Deeper and deeper into the woods they drove, crunching through the bracken.

Eventually, when the trees had become so thick it was almost dark, Mr. Goldtail turned off the engine and let out a deep sigh.

"Well, I reckon we've gotten away all right," he said. "They'll never find us now."

302

"We'll have to be more careful in the future," Mr. Mirth said. "I wonder how they found out about us. I didn't think the word would spread so fast."

"Found out *what?*" the General asked. "Oh, *please* will someone tell me what's going on? Who were we running away from? Who was blowing that whistle so loudly?"

The others looked at him coldly.

"*Who?*" Mr. Goldtail sneered. "Why, the policemice, of course! We can recognize their whistles from a mile away. I don't know how many of them there were — there might have been only one, but there might have been half a dozen of them, running up on us through the grass. We weren't going to take any chances. If we'd hung around a minute longer, we'd have been arrested!"

"*Arrested?*" the General gasped. "But why? What have we done?"

Mr. Mirth gave a nasty cackle. "Haven't you guessed what our game is by now, General? We're not *real* circus mice. The ticket booth and the big top — they're just a cover-up. Our real job is BURGLING MOUSE HOLES. That's what we do for a living!"

"Burgling m——*Good grief!*" the General stammered. He was too horrified to speak.

Mr. Moody jerked a paw over his shoulder. "In those wagons back there, we've got more gold and silver than you've ever set eyes on!" he said proudly. "We're going to sell it when we get to London, and we'll all be rich!"

"London?" the General gasped.

"That's right," Mr. Goldtail said. "It's a long way, but we reckon we'll get there in a month or two——especially now that we've got this nice fast bus to drive. And there'll be lots of rich mouse holes to burgle on the way!"

The General was appalled. He thought he had joined a circus——but instead he had fallen in with a gang of common thieves!

"I am leaving!" he said, flinging open the door. "And when I see those policemice, I shall tell them which way you've gone!"

"Oh, but I wouldn't be so hasty if I were you, General," Mr. Goldtail said mockingly. "You don't want to be caught by the police any more than we do!"

The General snorted. "I'm not a thief!" he fumed. "I've nothing to fear from the police!"

"Ha! What do you think the policemice will say when we tell them that you've stolen a bus?" Mr. Goldtail snarled. "You've supplied the getaway vehicle, General. You're as much a crook as we are! If the police catch us, you'll go to prison, too."

"How ridiculous! I only borrowed the bus—I didn't steal it!" the General said furiously. "Now let me out!"

He turned to the door and started to lower himself to the ground.

"Get back in your seat," Mr. Goldtail growled. His voice was ice cold—and when the General turned around, he saw that he had whipped out a gun.

"Close the door!" Mr. Goldtail barked, pointing the nozzle straight at the General's nose. "This gun's loaded with sherbet."

The General gulped, for as he knew very well, sherbet guns are horrid things. They are loaded with a sickly yellow powder, which comes shooting out in a choking blast. If a mouse is hit by one at close range, the sherbet burns his throat and stings his eyes, and turns his stomach into lemonade.

He squirmed back into his seat and pulled shut the door.

Mr. Goldtail passed the gun to Mr. Mirth and started the engine. The bus gave a sputter and lurched on through the woods.

The General was numb with fear. And it was not just the gun he was afraid of. The others were right—when the police found out he had taken Arthur's bus, they would think he was a thief, too. He would be stripped of his medals and sent to prison. Oh, the shame of it! The shame!

"Don't look so glum, General," Mr. Goldtail sneered. "You do as we say and we'll make sure you're all right. You can help us rob the village shop!"

"*The village shop?*" the General said feebly.

"That's right," Mr. Moody said. "We're going to bust in after closing time, and gorge ourselves on ice-cream cakes and jam tarts! And we'll steal all the tubes of sherbet to use in our guns!"

"And no one will catch us now that we've got this speedy bus to escape in!" Mr. Mirth gloated. "We'll be able to carry out twice the number of robberies now! And it's all thanks to you, General!"

"Three cheers for General Marchmouse!" Mr. Merry cried.

"Hip hip hooray! Hip hip hooray! Hip hip hooray!"

The General sat silently in the backseat. He could hear the joyless cheers echoing around him, as if in a terrible dream. He thought of his wife, and of Tumtum and Nutmeg, and of all the army medals for which he had fought so bravely . . . but they seemed lost in a distant past.

Oh, if only he hadn't borrowed the wretched bus! But he had gone too far to turn back. . . . He was a criminal now.

## Chapter Eight

Meanwhile, back at Rose Cottage, Arthur and Lucy had been looking for the bus all morning.

They had searched the garden twice, and they had gone up and down the little lane that ran in front of Rose Cottage, peeking under the parked cars and poking along the ditch.

But by lunchtime there was still no sign of it.

"Whoever stole it has probably driven out of the village by now," Arthur said as they came back inside. "I bet we'll *NEVER* get it back. And we'll never discover who the mysterious thief was either!"

They sat down to lunch feeling very glum. They did not say anything to their father about the missing bus, for they suspected he would not believe such a peculiar story. And this was *their* adventure — they didn't want any grown-ups interfering before they'd had a chance to solve it themselves.

Mr. Mildew spent the whole meal with his head buried in a book, so it was easy to exclude him from the conversation.

"I think we should write to Nutmeg and tell her everything that's happened. I bet she'll know who took the bus, and perhaps she'll be able to help us find it," Lucy said.

Arthur nodded. Lucy was right. This was just the sort of mystery Nutmeg might be able to solve. So as soon as lunch was finished, they hurried upstairs to write her a letter.

But when they walked into the attic, they got a big surprise — for Nutmeg had already been there. And she had left a letter for *them*! It was in the usual place, propped up against Lucy's hairbrush on top of the chest of drawers.

"Quick, let's see what it says," Arthur said excitedly. "Perhaps she knows about the bus already!"

Lucy grabbed the magnifying glass from her bedside table, then sat down on her bed, holding the letter in her palm.

"Oh, hurry!" Arthur cried impatiently. "What does it say?"

Lucy was squinting. "It looks like Nutmeg wrote it in a

great hurry—her writing's even more squiggly than usual!"
she said. Eventually, stumbling a little, she managed to read it
out loud:

*URGENT*

*Dear Arthur and Lucy,*

*Last night your toy bus was borrowed by a mischievous*
*friend of mine. He only took it for a bit of fun, and I'm sure*
*he intended to bring it back. But now the strangest thing*
*has happened, for he has fallen in with a real circus, which*
*is camped down in the meadow! And they plan to run away*
*to London together, traveling in YOUR BUS!*

*But you can stop them! You should go down to the*
*meadow at once, my dears, and snatch the bus back! You will*
*find it parked on the bank of the stream, beside the willow*
*tree. Now hurry, for they plan to set off this afternoon!*

*Love,*

*Nutmeg*

The children were astonished.

"A friend of Nutmeg! But who could that be?" Arthur asked. "And I wonder who the *real* circus belongs to."

"Perhaps it's a fairy's circus!" Lucy said.

Arthur scrunched his nose. He did not believe in fairies, except for Nutmeg, of course. And she was a Fairy of Sorts, which was different. "Perhaps it's a rat circus!" he said eagerly. "Now *that* would be exciting!"

"Rats! Ugh! I hope not!" Lucy shuddered.

"Well, whoever they are, we've got to stop them before they take my bus to London," Arthur cried, leaping up from the bed.

The children set off at once. They ran across the garden and clambered over the gate, wondering what on earth they were going to find.

But the mystery was not going to be solved as soon as they had hoped, for General Marchmouse's adventure had just taken a turn for the worse.

# Chapter Nine

The children ran across the meadow until they were in sight of the stream. Then they stopped still and stood peering along the bank. They could see the willow tree, but the ground around it was hidden by ferns.

They crept up to it on tiptoe, hoping to take the circus by surprise. But when they reached the tree and searched all around it, the circus wasn't there!

"Nutmeg must have gotten the wrong tree," Arthur said impatiently. "Come on, we'll have to look all along the bank. It must be here somewhere!"

He ran back to the stream and started poking around in the bushes. Lucy was about to follow him, but then she noticed something curious on the ground. To one side of the willow tree, there was a patch of grass that had been flattened, as though a bucket had been placed on it. And in the middle of it, she could see something glowing.

She wondered if it might be a bead, or a gold coin. But then she noticed little feathers of smoke rising from it. And when she knelt down and peered at it more closely, she saw that it was a tiny campfire, and lying on the grass next to it was a frying pan the size of a penny.

"Arthur, quick! Come and look at this!" she cried.

She held the pan in the palm of her hand, and they both studied it in astonishment.

"Yuck!" Arthur said. "It's got a burnt fly in it!"

"And look at the fire!" Lucy said, pointing to the tiny pile of smoldering twigs. "This must be where the circus was parked. You can see where the grass has been flattened by the wagons and the big top!"

"So Nutmeg was right. The circus was here!" Arthur cried. "But we're too late. It's gone!"

"Well, they wouldn't have gotten far," Lucy said. "Their campfire's still burning, which means they can't have left long ago. But I wonder which way they went."

Then Arthur noticed something else. "Look here!" he said, pointing to two little tracks weaving through the grass. "These must be the marks made by the wheels of the bus and the wagons."

"Well spotted!" Lucy said. "If we follow these, then we're sure to find them!"

They jumped up excitedly and followed the trail along the grass by the bank of the stream. But when they reached the edge of the meadow, the ground turned to bare earth, and the tracks disappeared.

"Oh no!" Arthur said. "Now what do we do?"

"Well, they can't have crossed the stream — there's no bridge," Lucy said. "They must have driven into the woods."

"Then we'll never find them!" Arthur said glumly. "The woods are huge and full of bracken."

"Yes, but if you go straight through it, you come out behind the church," Lucy said. "Well, I bet that's what they've done. If they plan to drive all the way to London, they'll have to get

316

onto a proper road at some stage. So they'll probably cut down through the church, and then on to one of the lanes leading out of the village."

"All right, then," Arthur said. "Let's see if we can find them on the road."

They clambered over the gate at the bottom of the meadow and followed the footpath along the edge of the woods until they reached the churchyard. Then they ran up the path to the gate and let themselves out onto the lane.

To the right, the lane forked in two, with both ways weaving into the open countryside. To the left, it led past the war memorial and the village shop, then back toward Rose Cottage.

"Which way's London?" Arthur said.

"Let's go to the shop and ask Mrs. Paterson," Lucy suggested. "She's sure to know."

They hurried along, for it was nearly teatime, and the shop would be closing soon.

But just as they were crossing the lane toward it, Lucy suddenly stopped. "Arthur, look!" she whispered. "*Over there!*"

She was pointing to the side of the shop, where the trash cans were kept.

"What is it?" Arthur asked.

"It was the bus!" Lucy said. "I just saw it, really I did—it went racing off behind those trash cans! And it was towing lots of wagons!"

Arthur looked doubtful. He wondered why he hadn't seen it, too. But they would know soon enough if Lucy had been imagining things. "Come on, let's go and have a look," he said. "The alley's a dead end. If the bus did go down there, then we're sure to find it!"

They crossed the lane and ran around to the side of the shop. The alley was very short, but it was full of trash cans and cardboard boxes, so it took them a while to dig around. And just as Arthur was peering under a box, Mrs. Paterson appeared. She had just closed the shop for the day, and now she was carrying out the trash.

"Whatever are you doing here?" she asked the children in surprise.

"Er, I was . . . looking for something I'd lost," Arthur mumbled. "A . . . um . . . well, a toy bus actually!"

"Well, I'll let you know if I see it!" Mrs. Paterson said. "Now, shouldn't you be getting home? It will be dark soon. Your father will be worrying about you."

"Yes, we're just going back now," Arthur said, for he didn't want Mrs. Paterson interfering in their secret search. "And, er . . . one thing, Mrs. Paterson. Do you know which way London is?"

"London? Well, it'll be about a hundred miles that way." Mrs. Paterson tutted, pointing up the lane toward the church. "Why, are you planning to run away?"

"Oh, no . . . we were just, well . . . just wondering," Lucy said hurriedly. "Anyway, we'd better be getting home."

The children said goodbye, then they turned and headed back toward Rose Cottage.

"Are you *sure* you saw it?" Arthur said.

"Quite sure! How many times do I have to tell you?" Lucy replied impatiently. "It drove behind the cans, then it just sort of . . . vanished!"

"Well, if you're sure you saw it, then we'll have to go back first thing in the morning and have another look," Arthur said. "It can't just have disappeared. Maybe it's hiding under one of those cardboard boxes, though I'm sure I looked under them all."

"Yes, let's go back after breakfast," Lucy said. "You know, I feel *sure* we're going to find it!"

But the morning was still a long way off. There was the whole night to get through first, and all sorts of mysterious things were going to happen.

# Chapter Ten

Tumtum and Nutmeg had spent an anxious afternoon in Nutmouse Hall, waiting for the children to come back from the meadow. But by teatime there was still no sound of them.

"They should have been home *ages* ago—it couldn't have taken them more than half an hour to run down to the stream and back," Nutmeg said anxiously. "Whatever could have happened?"

"Perhaps we had better go and look for them," Tumtum said. But just as they were getting ready to go out, they heard a door slam, and then the thunder of feet in the kitchen.

"Oh, thank goodness! That must be them!" Nutmeg said.

They hurried out of their front gates and crept to the edge

of the dresser. The children had just come in from the garden, and they still had their coats on. But when the Nutmouses saw that they had returned without the bus, they looked at each other in dismay.

"Whatever could have happened?" Nutmeg whispered. "Why didn't they bring it back?"

She and Tumtum crouched beneath the dresser, trying to find out what had gone wrong.

"I wish it would hurry up and be morning so we can go and have another look in that alley," Arthur said.

"It's a good thing tomorrow's Sunday and there's no school," Lucy said. "Let's go and write Nutmeg a letter, telling her everything that's happened."

"All right," Arthur said. "Just think how surprised she'll be when she learns that the circus has already gone!"

The children dashed upstairs, leaving Tumtum and Nutmeg in suspense.

"Gone? Oh, how dreadful!" Nutmeg cried. "But whatever could have happened? The children should have had plenty of time to snatch the bus before the circus set off!"

"Hmm. And I wonder what this alley is that they're referring to," Tumtum said.

"They're sure to explain everything in their letter," Nutmeg said. "We shall just have to wait until we can read it."

They did not dare follow the children up to the attic, for fear of being seen. So they waited impatiently under the dresser, until eventually Arthur and Lucy came downstairs. Lucy went into the pantry to find something for dinner, and Arthur went to put his bicycle in the shed.

The mice seized their chance. They shot out from beneath the dresser and dashed up the baseboard beside the stairs. Then they crossed the first-floor landing and slowly heaved themselves up the steep wooden steps to the attic.

When they finally crept into the children's bedroom, they saw a letter addressed to Nutmeg propped against the mirror on the chest of drawers.

They climbed up to it, clutching onto the tights and socks that had been left tumbling from the drawers.

Then they anxiously unfolded the letter and stood together at the bottom of the page, reading what it said:

*Dear Nutmeg,*

*We went straight down to the meadow, just as you told us to, but the circus had left! Then we thought we saw the bus on our way home, going down the alley at the side of the village shop. We tried to follow it, but we couldn't find it.... And then Mrs. Paterson appeared. But we'll go and look again in the morning.*

*Love,*

*Arthur and Lucy*

"The morning might be too late!" Nutmeg cried. "We shall have to go to the shop tonight and try to persuade the General to come back! Oh, I do hope the circus is still there!"

"Let's go back to Nutmouse Hall and fetch our coats and a flashlight, then we can set out straight away!" Tumtum said.

They climbed back to the floor and hurried downstairs. The children had moved into the living room, so they were able to dash back under the dresser unseen.

Then they ran back into Nutmouse Hall and put on their

warm clothes. But as they were about to leave the house, there was a sharp *Rap! Tap! Tap!* on the front door.

The Nutmouses looked at each other in surprise. They had not been expecting visitors tonight, and they wondered who it could be.

"Perhaps the General's come back!" Nutmeg said hopefully. But when Tumtum opened the door, they got a big surprise.

It was Mrs. Marchmouse. She looked very upset, and her nose was wet with tears.

"Mrs. Marchmouse!" Nutmeg said in astonishment. "We thought you were away looking after your sister—oh, goodness! Is she all right?"

But before Mrs. Marchmouse could speak, a second mouse appeared.

This time, Tumtum and Nutmeg were even more taken aback. For it was Chief Constable Watchmouse, the head of the local Mouse Police Station! His snowy whiskers glared against his black uniform, and his big red nose was twitching.

He stood twisting his baton in his paws, looking very grave.

"Mr. and Mrs. Nutmouse," he said, addressing them in his most solemn voice. "I believe you might be able to assist me in my investigation."

"Assist you in . . . *Gracious me!* What's all this about?" Tumtum said, looking very alarmed.

The Chief Constable cleared his throat, clearly relishing the drama. But before he could explain his business, Mrs. Marchmouse started sobbing out the story herself.

"Oh, Mr. and Mrs. Nutmouse, you will never guess what's happened!" she cried. "I came home early from my sister's mouse hole, seeing as she was so much better, and seeing as I was missing my poor Marchie so much. . . . But when I let myself in, there was the Chief Constable, *searching the gun cupboard!* And he's got A WARRANT FOR MY HUSBAND'S ARREST!"

Tumtum and Nutmeg were astounded.

"*A warrant for his arrest?* Whatever do you mean?" Tumtum asked.

"They say he's joined a gang of thieves!" Mrs. Marchmouse trembled. "Oh, tell me it's not true, Mr. Nutmouse! Tell me it's not true!"

"Gang of th——" Nutmeg stammered, hardly able to believe her ears.

"But, Chief Constable, there's been a terrible mistake!" Tumtum cried. "The General hasn't joined a gang of thieves. He's joined a circus! We went to see him! Now, I can assure you, this is all a misunderstanding!"

But Mrs. Marchmouse did not seem at all reassured. At the mention of the circus, she started sobbing even harder.

The Chief Constable raised his baton, gesturing for them to stay calm.

"The information I have is that General Marchmouse has joined Mr. Goldtail's circus," he said. "Or should I say, Mr. Goldtail's circus that is *pretending* to be a circus…but that is not really a circus at all!"

"*Not* a circus? But what do you mean, Chief Constable?" Tumtum asked, finding this all very confusing. "They must be a circus—they've got wagons and a big top!"

"Ha!" The Chief Constable snorted. "You weren't the first to be fooled by all that, Mr. Nutmouse! But I tell you, those wagons and that tent are just a front! Mr. Goldtail and his gang don't have one single drop of *real* circus blood in their tails!"

"But then who are they?" Nutmeg asked.

"They are *WANTED CRIMINALS*," the Chief Constable announced dramatically. "Burglars, Mrs. Nutmouse—and very accomplished ones, too. They have robbed more mouse holes than you've eaten cockroach pies! Their wagons aren't used for carrying circus insects—they're used for carrying *stolen goods*!"

Nutmeg clapped her paw to her mouth in horror. No wonder the circus had given her such funny feelings! *They were thieves!* The cardboard boxes that she and Tumtum had seen stacked high in the second wagon must have been full of all the things they had stolen. And the silver in the General's wagon must have been stolen, too! And to think that the poor General had been fooled by them!

"But why aren't they behind bars?" Tumtum asked.

"Because they are VERY CUNNING," the Chief Constable replied. "We call them the Vanishing Circus: here one minute—and gone the next! I'll tell you how they operate, Mr. Nutmouse. They turn up somewhere quite out of the blue—somewhere they've never been before, where the local mice don't know how wicked they are. Then they quickly put up some posters and put on a show. And very poor shows they are, from all I've heard—no trapeze, no dragonflies, just an old beetle! But the field mice all go because it's not every day a mouse circus comes by—and of course, they don't know how rotten the show's going to be until it's begun."

"What about the clowns?" Tumtum interrupted.

"The clowns? Ha! That's the whole business!" The Constable grunted. "Only one of the clowns performs in each show. The other two sneak out when the field mice are in their seats and burgle their mouse holes. And by the time everyone gets home and discovers they've been robbed, the circus has packed up and gone!"

"How shocking!" Nutmeg cried.

"But now the law's catching up with them," the Chief Constable said confidently. "The last set of burglaries they carried out were on Apple Farm, less than two miles away! So the police station down there sent me a telegram, warning me they might be coming this way!"

"Why haven't you arrested them?" Tumtum asked.

"Oh, believe me, I've tried!" the Chief Constable said. "When I heard they'd arrived in the meadow, I rushed straight there. But they must have gotten wind I was coming, because by the time I reached their campsite, they were gone! But I saw one of their posters tacked to a fern stem. And imagine my surprise when I saw that General Marchmouse was topping the bill!"

"But it must be a mistake!" Mrs. Marchmouse wept. "Why would he want to get mixed up with wicked mice like that?"

Tumtum and Nutmeg agreed that there must have been a terrible misunderstanding.

"Now listen here, Chief Constable," Tumtum said firmly. "We spoke to the General this morning, and he had *no idea* that Mr. Goldtail was a crook. He thought the circus was real, just like we did. And he only joined it for a bit of fun. He'll change his mind soon enough when he finds out they're burglars! I wouldn't be surprised if he doesn't try to arrest them himself!"

But the Chief Constable did not look convinced. "I have

been reliably informed, Mr. Nutmouse," he said, "that the circus is traveling in a stolen bus. And last night, near the hour of seven o'clock, the General was seen driving that *very same* bus at considerable speed across the garden of Rose Cottage."

The Chief Constable paused to allow this dramatic information to sink in. "I have three different field mice who will back up that version of events," he added solemnly. "So it would appear, Mr. Nutmouse, that the General has not only teamed up with Mr. Goldtail and his gang . . . he has supplied them with a getaway vehicle!"

Tumtum and Nutmeg looked horrified.

"But Chief Constable," Tumtum said, "this is quite unfair. It's true that the General took the bus last night — but he only meant to *borrow* it. He's borrowed the children's toys before, but he's always given them back! And he wouldn't have driven anywhere near that wicked circus-that-isn't-a-circus if he knew what sort of mice they were."

The Chief Constable hesitated. He agreed that borrowing was not the same as stealing. Even so, the General had a lot to answer for. "He must have found out by now that Mr. Goldtail

334

and his mice are crooks—they've been on the run all afternoon," he said. "So why hasn't he come home?"

"They're probably holding him against his will," Tumtum said. "They'll be frightened that if they let him go, he'll come and tell you where they are!"

"That's right!" Nutmeg cried. "And I bet they think that when they reach London, his famous name will attract more visitors to their shows!"

"Holding him against his will! Oh, how awful!" Mrs. Marchmouse sobbed.

But the Chief Constable was still not convinced. "So long as the General is on the run, he remains under suspicion," he said firmly. "The important thing is to catch these criminals—*then* we can decide whether the General's guilty or not. But I've already searched the village high and low!"

"But *we* know which way they went!" Nutmeg said. "The children left us a letter just before you arrived saying that they saw them disappearing down the alley beside the village shop!"

"The village shop!" the Chief Constable exclaimed. "Well,

well, I can guess why they've gone there. They'll be doing a break-in, I bet!"

Everyone gasped. "But surely they're not planning to rob Mrs. Paterson!" Nutmeg said in horror.

"Oh, yes! Believe me, Mrs. Nutmouse, that is just the sort of mice they are!" the Chief Constable replied. "They'll dig into her ice-cream cakes, and steal all the gold coins from her cash register! COME ON! Let's go and catch them red-handed!"

## Chapter Eleven

The Chief Constable was longing to make an arrest. Mr. Goldtail was one of the most wanted mice in the country, so it was thrilling to think he might catch up with him at last.

"I shall set off at once!" he said gleefully, bounding from the door.

"But you'll never catch them on foot!" Tumtum cried. "Not if they're in a bus. You must take Arthur's police car!"

"*A police car!*" the Chief Constable exclaimed. "Does he have one? A *real* one, with a siren and an accelerator and a flashing light?"

"He certainly does," Tumtum replied. "It's parked just outside in the kitchen, behind the vegetable rack. I saw it there this afternoon. And it's a splendid car, I can tell you!

Nutmeg and I had a test-drive in it one night, and it went at a speedy pace!"

"That's right!" Nutmeg said excitedly. "We'll come with you—there's plenty of room for us all to ride inside."

The Chief Constable's face glowed. He had always longed for a police car of his own, but the Mouse Police Force only provided cars for officers in the city.

"Are you sure the children won't mind us using it?" he asked anxiously.

"Of course not," Tumtum replied. "We'll leave them a note, explaining that we've borrowed it in order to arrest Mr. Goldtail and rescue their bus."

Everyone agreed that it was an excellent plan.

"We must hurry," Nutmeg said anxiously. "Mr. Mildew usually takes out the trash after dinner. When he opens the back door, that will be our chance to drive the car outside!"

Nutmeg went to the living room and hastily scribbled a letter to the children. Then she tucked it into her pocket, and they all hurried out of Nutmouse Hall.

The kitchen was deserted, but a light had been left on, and

when they peered across the floor, they could just see the police car's yellow hood shining behind the vegetable rack.

They crept over to it. And when the Chief Constable saw the car, he gave a whoop of joy. It was longer and sleeker than he could ever have dreamed, and it had a big blue siren and a walkie-talkie!

He tugged open the driver's door, his heart pounding with glee. But then he suddenly jumped back in fear.

"Who's *that*?" he cried, pointing to the backseat.

Tumtum and Nutmeg laughed. "Oh, that's nothing to be frightened of! It's only Arthur's toy policeman!" Nutmeg said.

"Goodness me!" the Chief Constable said, for it looked very fierce. It was sitting in the backseat, holding a pistol and a pair of handcuffs.

"He's a mechanical toy," Tumtum explained. "When you wind him up, he marches along, shouting, 'Stop where you are, you are under arrest!' He makes Lucy's dolls tremble!"

"Let's take him with us," the Chief Constable said eagerly. "He'll frighten the wits out of Mr. Goldtail!"

"Where shall I leave the letter?" Nutmeg wondered. "I haven't time to go and deliver it to the attic."

"I've an idea," Tumtum said. "Why don't you leave it on Arthur's shoe? He always wears that pair that's on the doormat, so he'll find your letter when he puts them on in the morning."

"Good idea," Nutmeg said, and she ran over and tucked the letter into one of the laces.

Then they all jumped into the car. Tumtum sat in the front next to the Chief Constable, and Nutmeg and Mrs. Marchmouse squeezed into the back, on either side of the toy policeman.

They waited silently. They didn't dare start the engine, for fear someone might hear.

Eventually, they felt the whole floor tremble, and when they peered up out of the windshield they saw Mr. Mildew striding in. They all sat still as stone, watching as he switched on the kettle, then started clattering some dishes in the sink.

Finally, he stooped down and heaved the bag out of the trash can, then turned and pulled open the back door.

"Get ready!" Tumtum whispered.

The Chief Constable turned the key in the ignition, and the engine gave a gentle purr. They waited until Mr. Mildew had walked a little way down the path, toward where the cans were kept.

"Quick, go now!" Tumtum cried.

The Chief Constable pressed forward the gearshift, and the car glided across the kitchen floor and slipped out the doorway.

Mr. Mildew was heaving the trash into the cans as the toy car slunk past behind him. The Chief Constable drove slowly, fearful of making too much noise. It was only when they had swung out onto the lane that he dared to slam down his paw on the accelerator. Then off they sped, with their siren wailing.

The village was dark and still. The fires had been lit, and the televisions were flickering behind the curtains. No one saw the little toy car racing toward the village shop.

Nutmeg and Mrs. Marchmouse clung to their seats, for the Chief Constable was driving at a terrifying speed. When they reached the shop, he screeched to a halt. The shutters had been

pulled down, and there was a CLOSED sign hanging from the door. But there was light coming from the windows of Mrs. Paterson's flat, on the floor above.

"Try down the alley," Tumtum said. "That's where the children thought they saw them."

The Chief Constable sped around the side of the building. They came into a forest of crates and trash cans towering ghoulishly in the moonlight.

They raced all around them, skidding and looping. Round and round they went, searching behind every box and bin. But the circus bus wasn't there.

The Chief Constable thumped the steering wheel in frustration. "We're too late!" he said furiously. "The scoundrels have gone!"

"They must have left for London already!" Mrs. Marchmouse sobbed. "Now I'll never get my husband back!"

Everyone felt wretched. But then Tumtum noticed something in the headlights. "Hey, look over there!" he said, pointing ahead. "That's where they must have broken in!"

They all peered through the windshield. The Chief

343

Constable had stopped the car at the bottom of the alley, beside a tall thin door leading into the back of the shop. The door was made of glass, and the bottom pane had been broken. The hole was just big enough for a mouse to get through!

"Ha! So they *did* break in, as I suspected!" the Chief Constable said. "I shall go inside and take some paw prints."

He grabbed his baton, then turned to Tumtum and flung him a pair of handcuffs. "Come on, Mr. Nutmouse!" he said. "Let's see if they're still in there."

Tumtum clambered nervously out of the car.

"Don't forget the toy policeman!" Nutmeg said, for she was frightened Mr. Goldtail and his gang might become aggressive.

Nutmeg and Mrs. Marchmouse jumped out and helped Tumtum drag the policeman from the backseat.

They turned him around, so that he was facing the door of the shop, then Tumtum took hold of the silver knob on his back, and wound it in three full circles.

The policeman shuffled his feet, and his eyes rolled in their sockets. "Stick 'em up!" he cried. "You are under arrest!"

Then the policeman marched forward and smashed through the broken pane of glass. Tumtum and the Chief Constable scrambled after him, while Nutmeg and Mrs. Marchmouse waited anxiously outside.

It was very dark inside the shop. All they could see was the outline of a pile of pie shells towering in front of them. They crept around it, with the policeman marching alongside. Then they took out their flashlights and shone them around.

They both gasped, for the shop was in a terrible mess. On every shelf, packets of chips and cookies and jam tarts had been gnawed open, and candy wrappers nibbled to shreds.

"Come out, wherever you are!" the Chief Constable shouted. "Do you hear me? This is the police! Come out with your paws above your heads!"

"Stick 'em up! Stick 'em up!" the toy policeman squeaked.

There was not a sound.

"Drat, they've gone!" the Chief Constable muttered. "But what's happened to the General?" Tumtum said. "He would *never* have assisted in a burglary like this. They must be holding him against—"

345

But then the Chief Constable shone his flashlight onto the cake shelf and gave his whistle a piercing shrill. And when Tumtum spun around he saw the most astonishing sight.

It was General Marchmouse, trapped in a chocolate éclair! What a sight he looked. He was sunk in it up to his waist, and it was so sticky he couldn't get out. His gold suit was covered in goop, and he looked very embarrassed.

"Come down with your paws above your head! You are under arrest!" the Chief Constable shouted.

"I can't come down. Can't you see? I'm stuck!" the General replied, blushing furiously. "Now get me out of here. The burglary had nothing to do with me. All I did was borrow a silly old bus!"

Hearing the commotion, Nutmeg and Mrs. Marchmouse came running in from outside. When she saw her husband, Mrs. Marchmouse let out a cry of relief—but she could see there was a lot of explaining to be done.

"Get me down! My boots are soaking!" the General cried.

The Chief Constable stared at him coldly. The evidence looked very bad. But Tumtum still could not believe that the

General had been part of the burglary. "Let's get him down and hear what he has to say," he said.

He and the Chief Constable climbed up to the shelf, and between the two of them they pulled General Marchmouse out of the éclair and helped him down to the floor.

"All right, then, General," the Chief Constable said gruffly. "What's been going on here?"

"Oh, Constable!" the General spluttered. "I have been treated most hideously! Mr. Goldtail and his gang forced me to come in here and help them load up their wagons with stolen sherbet. And they said that if I didn't do as I was told, they'd throw me in the licorice jar and leave me there for Mrs. Paterson to find in the morning!

"But I escaped by bravely burrowing inside a chocolate sponge cake. They hunted high and low for me, but I was too well hidden. You should have heard them cursing! Anyway, I waited until they'd left, then I crawled out, and I was going to come straight to the station to tell you what had happened. But I didn't have a flashlight, and I stepped into an éclair! And now everyone will think I'm a criminal, just because I borrowed

Arthur's bus. . . . But I only borrowed it for a bit of fun! And it was my birthday, after all."

Tumtum and Nutmeg and Mrs. Marchmouse could tell at once that the General was telling the truth. He had been very wrong to take Arthur's bus. But it was clear that he had been horribly fooled by Mr. Goldtail and his gang.

They looked anxiously at the Chief Constable, wondering if he would believe the General, too.

The Chief Constable was scratching his chin.

"You have been a very foolish mouse, General," he said eventually. "And next time you borrow a toy bus without permission I might not be so lenient! But for now you have been punished enough."

Tumtum and Nutmeg and Mrs. Marchmouse looked very relieved. "Oh, thank goodness!" Mrs. Marchmouse cried.

The General was relieved, too, for he had feared he might go to prison. But he was too proud to let his gratitude show.

"Well, I'm glad that's cleared up, then," he said briskly. "Now I can go home and have a hot bath."

"Not so fast, General," the Chief Constable said. "We need

to catch this gang, and FAST. Have you any idea where they went?"

"Well, yes. Now that you mention it, I think I do," the General replied.

"*Where?*" the Chief Constable asked excitedly.

Everyone looked at the General, waiting to hear what he would say. There was an atmosphere of great suspense. The General knew his news would come as a big surprise, and he started to feel rather important.

He brushed a blob of cream off his jacket, trying to look more as a general should.

"I regret to inform you," he announced dramatically, "but Mr. Goldtail and his gang have GONE TO BURGLE NUT-MOUSE HALL!"

# Chapter Twelve

Everyone gasped.

"They've gone to burgle Nutmouse Hall!" Nutmeg cried. "Oh, my, oh, my! They'll take our family portraits and our silver candlesticks and our crystal glasses and our gold goblets and our stuffed ladybugs and our rare books and . . . and . . ."

She clapped a paw to her mouth, too upset to continue. Tumtum was distraught, too.

"Have they gone straight there?" he asked anxiously.

"No, the burglary's planned for tomorrow evening," the General replied. "They've got to do some repair work first on their wagons."

"Where are they tonight?" the Chief Constable asked.

"I couldn't really tell," the General replied. "Mr. Goldtail just said, 'Okay, let's camp under the rhubarb again!' and the clowns all agreed with him. Well, I didn't want to ask which rhubarb he meant, for fear of making him suspicious. Mr. Goldtail doesn't like being asked questions, you know."

"*The rhubarb*," the Chief Constable said thoughtfully. "Hmm, that could be anywhere. The village is full of rhubarb—just about every garden has got some. We could search all night and still not find them. We shall have to wait until tomorrow and catch them when they go to Nutmouse Hall."

Everyone agreed that it was pointless looking for the thieves now. "You must all spend the night with us," Nutmeg said firmly. "We've plenty of food, and we can all drive home together in Arthur's car."

"An excellent plan," the Chief Constable said. He lived alone, and he would be glad to have some company after such an eventful day. The General was pleased, too, for he didn't want to walk home knowing that Mr. Goldtail and his gang were still lurking in the village.

Nutmeg was glad to have guests to fuss over. It would take her mind off all the worrying things that had been taking place.

"Now, let's see," she said. "I shall put the General and Mrs. Marchmouse in the green bedroom . . . and the Chief Constable can have the blue bedroom, next to ours and . . ."

*THUD!*

Everyone froze.

*THUD!*

It was footsteps on the stairs! Then suddenly the door behind the shop counter burst open, and on went the lights!

"It's Mrs. Paterson," Tumtum cried. "*RUN!*"

They all fled to the door, and scrambled out through the broken pane of glass. They could hear Mrs. Paterson shrieking behind them. "Help! Help! I've been robbed!"

"Quick! Get into the car!" the Chief Constable shouted. They all jumped in, the General squeezing between Nutmeg and Mrs. Marchmouse in the back. Then the Chief Constable revved the engine, and off they sped, tearing back toward Rose Cottage.

The passengers all peered anxiously through the back windshield, frightened that Mrs. Paterson might come running after them.

"Do you think she saw us?" Nutmeg asked.

"I don't think so," Tumtum said. "We were very quick — we got out before she came in. And if she had seen us, she'd have come chasing after us by now."

"Doesn't this feel strange?" Mrs. Marchmouse said nervously. "Here we are, running away as though *we* were the criminals!"

"Hmm, isn't it a pity humans can't hear what mice say?" Tumtum said. "Otherwise we could have told Mrs. Paterson the whole story."

As it was, they all felt very glad they had gotten away. For if Mrs. Paterson had seen them, she would have suspected *they* had made all the mess — and they dreaded to think what she would have done if she had caught them.

The Chief Constable did not stop until he reached Rose Cottage. Then he parked beside the garden door, and they crept back inside.

It was late now, and the Mildews had all gone up to bed. The kitchen was very dark. Tumtum led them across the floor with his flashlight and let them into Nutmouse Hall.

They were all very shaken. But they felt better when they had had something to eat. Nutmeg warmed up the cockroach soufflé she had made for the General's birthday feast, and everyone ate hungrily. They washed it down with a strong pot of tea. Nutmeg did not offer them the birthday cake or the strawberry pie or the jellied flies—the mood was not festive enough for party food.

Everyone was very worried about tomorrow. The General was the only one who felt talkative, and the others were too tired to stop him.

"So there we were, speeding off through the bracken yesterday afternoon—and I had no idea what was going on!" he recalled. "Then the scoundrels came clean and told me they were thieves! Well, you should have seen the fuss I made! 'Stop the bus!' I cried, 'I am going to get out and report you to the police!' But believe me, if they didn't tie me up and gag me...But I struggled as bravely as I could....."

On and on he boasted, though his memory was a little flawed. "...So imagine my relief when you finally arrived in the village shop," he said. "Though I can tell you, I got quite a fright when I saw that toy police—"

"*Oh, no!*" Nutmeg cried, dropping her fork with a clang. "The toy policeman! *WE FORGOT HIM!*"

Everyone groaned. It was true. In their haste to escape, they had left the policeman behind in the shop.

"Oh, well, there's nothing we can do about it now," the Chief Constable said. "And the shop's in such a mess. I'll bet Mrs. Paterson doesn't even notice the policeman tonight. I'll drive over there first thing in the morning and see if I can sneak in and get him back."

"All right," Tumtum said, feeling a little reassured. "Well, I suggest we get some sleep. We've a big day tomorrow, and we shall need to be alert."

Everyone agreed, for they were very tired. Even the General was fading. His eyes had become heavy, and he suddenly hadn't the strength to go on boasting.

Tumtum bolted the front door and locked all the windows. Then Nutmeg showed the guests to their rooms, and they were asleep almost as soon as they had pulled up the covers.

Tumtum fell asleep right away, too. But Nutmeg lay awake worrying. How she wished they hadn't left the toy policeman behind. She felt sure it would lead to trouble. And the next morning her fears were confirmed.

For as the mice breakfasted in Nutmouse Hall, they heard the Mildews' doorbell ringing, so loud it made them jump.

"I wonder who it could be, calling so early on a Sunday morning," Nutmeg said.

They stopped eating and sat with their ears twitching. They heard Mr. Mildew's footsteps coming down the cottage stairs, then a worried voice sounding from the hall.

Nutmeg recognized it at once. "It's Mrs. Paterson!" she said in alarm.

They tried to hear what she was saying. But then Mr. Mildew started talking at the same time, and the conversation became very difficult to follow.

Tumtum and Nutmeg left their guests at the table and crept out under the dresser to try and discover what was going on.

And when they peeked into the kitchen, they saw Mrs. Paterson standing by the table, clearly very upset. She had a wool coat pulled over her dressing gown, and her face was drained of color. In her hand was the toy policeman.

"I was burgled last night, Mr. Mildew. *Burgled!*" she cried. "Oh, you should see the mess! They gobbled my cupcakes and burst open the cornflakes! And they stole *all the sherbet!*"

Arthur and Lucy were standing by the kitchen table, looking very uncomfortable.

"Yes, Mrs. Paterson, I understand that, and I am very sorry," interrupted Mr. Mildew. He was wearing his robe, too, and looked a little bleary. "But I still don't quite see what you think we've got to do with it."

"I told you!" Mrs. Paterson cried, waving the toy policeman. "I found *this* lying on the floor, right next to my pie shells. And look, it's got Arthur's name scratched on it!" She turned the toy over, pointing to where the letters *A. Mildew* had been scratched out on the policeman's plastic back. "Your children must have crept in and dropped this while they were taking my sweets! They'd have had plenty of opportunity—I didn't lock the back door until after nine."

"But we didn't!" Arthur cried.

"Then how do you explain this?" Mrs. Paterson said, turning to wave the toy policeman at him. "And what were you doing snooping around my trash cans this afternoon?"

"Well, do you know anything about this?" Mr. Mildew asked the children. Nutmeg thought his tone was rather sharp.

Arthur and Lucy looked very awkward. They had found Nutmeg's letter earlier that morning, so they knew it was her who had taken their police car to the village shop.

But they didn't know what had happened next. Lucy tried to explain everything — or at least as much as they knew — even though she felt sure the grown-ups wouldn't believe her.

"On Friday night, Arthur's bus disappeared, and we looked everywhere, all over the garden, and all around the house, but we couldn't find it," she began. "Then yesterday afternoon, we thought we saw it driving down the little alley beside the shop. . . . And when we told our friend Nutmeg about it, she said she had discovered that the bus had been stolen by a gang of thieves, led by a wicked villain called Mr. Goldtail. . . . So she borrowed our toy police car and the policeman to go and arrest them, before they could do any more harm. . . . But the bus hasn't come back, and the toy policeman got left behind in your shop....So Nutmeg's whole mission must have gone wrong!"

"Oh, what nonsense!" Mrs. Paterson cried. "They're making fun of me!"

The children looked at their father anxiously. Surely *he* would believe them. But Mr. Mildew clearly thought it was ridiculous, too.

"This is no time for silly stories. You can see that Mrs. Paterson is upset," he said.

"But it's not a silly story. It's what happened! *It is!*" Arthur cried.

"That's enough," Mr. Mildew said sharply. "I want you both to go up to your room. And you can stay there until you're ready to discuss this sensibly — and tell me how the toy policeman really ended up in Mrs. Paterson's shop."

"Oh, Tumtum, what a terrible mess!" Nutmeg whispered. "The children are in trouble, and it's all our fault!"

"Come on," Tumtum said. "Let's hurry back to Nutmouse Hall and tell the others what's happened. We *must* catch Mr.

362

Goldtail tonight, otherwise the children will never clear their names!"

The mice hurried back into the broom cupboard. As they let themselves through the front gates, they heard Arthur and Lucy trudging upstairs.

The children felt miserable. It was terrible of their father to take Mrs. Paterson's side.

"Whatever could have happened?" Arthur said, flinging himself down on his bed. "I wonder why Nutmeg left the toy policeman behind."

"Well, she's brought the police car back," Lucy said. "I saw it outside on the doorstep. So at least Nutmeg must have gotten home safely. But I suppose Mr. Goldtail must have gotten away in the bus."

"Well, unless Nutmeg catches him, Mrs. Paterson will *never* believe our story," Arthur said wretchedly. "Oh, dear. Now *everything's* gone wrong!"

## Chapter Thirteen

Tumtum and Nutmeg hurried back to Nutmouse Hall to tell the others what had happened.

"Don't you worry, Mrs. Nutmouse," the Chief Constable said confidently. "I'll catch Mr. Goldtail and his good-for-nothing gang, and then the truth will come out!"

He took a pair of handcuffs from his bag and started polishing them with his napkin. It had been several weeks since he made an arrest, and he was very excited.

"I'll teach them what happens to mice who break into village shops!" he said fiercely. "I'll catch them red-handed when they turn up tonight!"

The Chief Constable checked his watch impatiently, wishing the evening would come.

But the General looked grumpy. He wanted to be in charge.

*This is* my *adventure,* he thought. *And that silly old policemouse has NO RIGHT to tell me what to do! I gave him the tip-off that Mr. Goldtail and his gang were coming to burgle Nutmouse Hall, so I should be allowed to arrest them all by myself!*

The General knew that the arrest of Mr. Goldtail would be reported in the *Mouse Times,* and he couldn't bear to think that the Chief Constable would get all the credit for it. *It should be* my *victory!* he thought.

Then suddenly he remembered something very important.

"You had better leave this arrest to me, Chief Constable," he said grandly. "It will need a general's expertise!"

The Chief Constable looked at him in astonishment. "Leave it to *you?* But you're not a policemouse!" he said indignantly. "This is my job!"

The General smiled smugly. "The problem is, I don't think you can handle this yourself," he said, "seeing as Mr. Goldtail and his gang have sherbet guns——"

"*SHERBET GUNS?*" the Chief Constable spluttered. "Are you sure?"

The General nodded. "They've got one each. They stocked up on powder when they broke into the village shop."

There was a stunned silence. They all knew how dangerous sherbet guns were.

"Oh, help us! What shall we do?" Mrs. Marchmouse cried.

"There is no need to fear," the General said bossily. "The Royal Mouse Army trained all its officers to deal with sherbet attacks. We shall be quite all right, so long as everyone does exactly what I say."

The Chief Constable looked furious. He could see that the General was trying to take command. "You are not telling me what to do!" he snapped.

"Oh, let's not bicker," Nutmeg said. "We must protect ourselves. Chief Constable, do you have any other policemice who might help us?"

The Chief Constable shook his head. "We're understaffed just now," he said. "My lieutenant's away on vacation, and my sergeant's out with the flu. We could summon reinforcements from the police station in town — they've got a dozen officers on duty. But it would take them two days to get here."

"And what about the Royal Mouse Army?" Tumtum asked.

"No good. The troops are down on Apple Farm, seeing off some rats from the hay barn," the General replied briskly. "We'd never be able to fetch them back in time."

"Well, then," Tumtum said anxiously. "It looks as if we're on our own."

"Indeed we are, but we can still win!" the General said with relish. "We must march up to the attic and borrow ammunition from Arthur's toy soldiers — guns, grenades, swords, all the weapons we can carry."

"All right, I'm sure Arthur won't mind," Tumtum said. "But there's to be no marching in Rose Cottage — when we go up to the attic, we shall have to sneak."

The General nodded. "And we shall need a toy tank, too," he said. "Have the children got one?"

"Yes!" Nutmeg cried. "There's one in the living room. It's been there for weeks, tucked behind the sofa. I think Arthur must have forgotten about it."

"Good," the Chief Constable said, trying to take control. "General, Tumtum — you can come with me after dark and drive it back to the kitchen. We can park behind the laundry basket, or somewhere the children won't see us. Then we'll take Mr. Goldtail and his gang by surprise as they sneak in under the garden door! Just think what a scare they'll get when they see an army tank zooming toward them!"

The Chief Constable was thrilled. Guns and tanks sounded much more fun than a baton.

"I'll drive!" the General said grandly. And the Chief Constable was too excited to argue.

So the plan was agreed upon, and the rest of the day was spent preparing for the attack. They intended to catch the thieves before they reached Nutmouse Hall, but even so, they didn't take any chances. Tumtum and the Chief Constable went all around the house, boarding up the doors and windows, and the General set trip wires in the living room and the butler's pantry. Nutmeg and Mrs. Marchmouse stuffed the chimneys with blankets and tapestries, in case they tried to drop sherbet bombs from the roof.

Lunch was a hasty affair, for they were all too nervous to eat much. As soon as the plates had been cleared, Tumtum and the General and the Chief Constable crept out into the kitchen and up to the attic to raid the toy barracks. They reappeared an hour later with toy guns and grenades thrust in their belts.

"Goodness, you do look fierce!" Mrs. Marchmouse said.

"Did you see the children?" Nutmeg asked anxiously.

"Yes, they are in the living room," Tumtum said. "So we won't be able to collect the tank yet—they'd be sure to see us. We shall have to wait until they go upstairs."

"And what about Mr. Mildew?" she asked.

"Oh, he's all right," Tumtum said. "He's shut away in his study. We could hear his typewriter keys clacking."

Nutmeg made a pot of tea, and they sat anxiously in the kitchen. Tumtum and the Chief Constable took turns to creep out of the broom cupboard to see if it was safe to go into the living room. But the children were milling about all afternoon.

Then Mr. Mildew came into the kitchen to make dinner. It

wasn't until nearly eight o'clock that the Chief Constable was able to report that everyone had gone upstairs.

"Come on, we must hurry up and get the tank!" the General said. "Mr. Goldtail might arrive at any minute!"

Tumtum and the General leaped up and followed him to the door.

"Oh, do be careful!" Nutmeg cried.

The mice crept out into the Mildews' kitchen. It was very dark. The lights were out, and they could see stars shining at the window.

Tumtum pulled out his flashlight and they set off toward the living room. But when they were halfway across the kitchen, they heard a sudden roar. And then there was a screech of brakes. The noise was coming from outside. And when they spun around they saw lights flashing under the back door!

"*It's them!*" the General hissed. "Quick! Hide!"

The mice darted behind a pile of telephone books. And when they peeked out, they saw four flashlights being shone around the floor.

"Keep back! Don't let them see us!" Tumtum hissed.

"Ha! Ha!" cried a nasty voice. "Let's go and blast Mr. Nutmouse with sherbet and steal all his valuables! We'll take his chandeliers and his silver candlesticks and his gold tapestries and his fancy soup bowls! Ha! Ha! We'll be as rich as can be!"

"That's Goldtail!" the General said grimly.

"Fetch the tank!" Tumtum whispered. "And HURRY!"

## Chapter Fourteen

Mr. Goldtail and his gang had never been to Rose Cottage before. They shone their flashlights around the kitchen, searching for the gates to Nutmouse Hall.

"Where are they?" Mr. Goldtail snarled. He grabbed a piece of paper from his pocket and read the address again.

Nutmouse Hall

The Broom Cupboard

The Kitchen

Rose Cottage

"Well, this is the kitchen. But I don't see a broom cupboard!"

"It must be here somewhere," said Mr. Moody. "Nutmouse Hall is the most famous mouse hole in the whole county."

"We've got to find it. I'm not leaving here empty-handed!" said Mr. Merry.

They continued to hunt, shining their flashlights around the baseboard.

Meanwhile, Tumtum, the General, and the Chief Constable crept out from behind the telephone books and tiptoed into the living room.

Tumtum was glad that Nutmouse Hall was so well hidden. But he knew the thieves would find it in the end.

"We must hurry," he whispered. "Imagine how frightened Nutmeg and Mrs. Marchmouse will be if they break in!"

One of the living room lamps had been left on, and they could just see the tank peeking out from behind the sofa.

They raced over to it. And when the General saw it up close, his eyes glinted. He had driven tanks in the Royal Mouse Army, but never one like this. It was as big as a cake pan and its gun was the size of a rattle!

Tumtum and the Chief Constable had never operated a

tank before, but the General reckoned he knew just what to do. He scrambled up the ladder and wrenched open the hatch. "Quick! Get in!" he shouted. Tumtum and the Chief Constable heaved themselves up after him. Then they all slid into the tank.

It was very dark inside. The General fumbled his way to the driver's seat and started blindly running his paws across the controls. There were dozens of buttons and switches. He felt about, pulling this one and that, until eventually a pale green light came on.

They all looked about them in surprise. They were in a small, gray cabin, and every wall was covered with switches, saying things like FIRE! and FULL SPEED! Everything was mouse-sized.

"Come on, General, let's go!" Tumtum cried, fearing that Nutmeg and Mrs. Marchmouse might be in danger.

The General slammed some more knobs on his dashboard, but he could not get the tank to start.

"Drat!" he said.

Then he saw a big red button labeled GO! He gave it a push. Finally the engine shuddered to life, and the tank ground forward across the carpet.

*Vroom!*

*Grrrrrrr!*

*Crrrrrrrrrrunch!*

The tank's huge rubber tracks bulldozed across a game of Snakes and Ladders, and over a discarded candy wrapper.

Tumtum and the Chief Constable crouched behind the General, peering through the bulletproof windshield.

"Straight ahead, left around the coffee-table leg, then hard right into the hall!" Tumtum said.

The General drove faster and faster, until finally they clattered into the kitchen.

"There they are!" the Chief Constable cried.

Mr. Goldtail and his mice were standing at the edge of the dresser, staring at the tank in astonishment.

"By Jove!" Tumtum said. "We got here just in time."

"Let's get them!" the General cried. The Chief Constable swung around the rotating gun until it was pointing toward the dresser.

They could see the thieves in the headlights, frantically loading their sherbet guns.

"Ha! They can't harm us with their silly old sherbet!" The General snorted. "We're in a sealed tank!"

But he spoke too soon. For at that moment the Chief Constable — who was quite senseless with excitement — leaped up and pushed open the hatch.

"Stop! What are you doing?" Tumtum cried. He tried to pull him back, but the Chief Constable was too fast. And before Tumtum could stop him, he poked out his head through the hatch and blew his whistle.

"Paws up! YOU ARE UNDER ARREST!" he cried.

"Get back, you fool!" the General shouted. But it was too late. For suddenly there was a deafening volley of gunfire, and a great blizzard of sherbet tore into the air. There was sherbet everywhere, swirling all around them. Soon the whole windshield was smothered.

The Chief Constable stumbled back inside the tank, gasping for air. He was covered with yellow powder from his ears to his chin, and his throat was burning.

The General leaped up and yanked down the hatch. But before he could shut it properly, a cloud of sherbet floated

down into the tank, turning the air a thick, dusty yellow. The General had his handkerchief clapped to his mouth. But Tumtum was taken unawares and started coughing violently.

"W-w-water!" he spluttered, collapsing beside the Chief Constable on the floor.

The General looked at them in horror. Tumtum's face had turned purple, and the Chief Constable was bright green.

The General knew that if he did not find them water, they would choke. He staggered about the tank, yanking the controls. "Water, water! A tank *must* have water!" he cried. But there was not a drop to be found.

Then, through the haze of sherbet, he saw a lever on the wall, with a sign reading PULL ONLY IN THE EVENT OF AN EXTREME EMERGENCY.

"This is an extreme emergency," he decided. And he grabbed it with both paws and wrenched it down.

Then something wonderful happened.

Three green sprinklers dropped down from the ceiling, and fierce jets of water whooshed out, washing all the sherbet away.

Tumtum and the Chief Constable struggled to their knees, raising their faces to the cool spray. The water stopped their coughing, but it was some moments before they could speak.

"Gracious! I thought we were done for!" Tumtum said weakly.

"Bah! I've survived far worse attacks than that in my Royal Mouse Army days," the General boasted. "Why, you should have seen the Battle of the —"

But he was cut short by another deafening rattle of gunfire, and then the next round of sherbet smacked against the tank.

"I'll show them not to fire their sherbet guns at me!" the General fumed. He flung himself back into the driver's seat and flicked on the windshield wipers. Then he rammed his paw on the accelerator. The tank surged forward, clattering across the tiled floor.

The General could see Mr. Goldtail and his accomplices in the headlights, and he drove straight at them.

The thieves hastily reloaded their guns, hoping to force the tank back with another blast of sherbet.

382

But while they were fumbling with their ammunition, the General swung around the tank's machine gun until it was pointing straight at them and thumped down his paw on a big red button marked FIRE!

All at once, a ferocious jet of water tore out of the nozzle of the gun and swept the thieves off their feet, rolling them across the floor like tennis balls.

"Ha! Ha! That'll teach you to fire sherbet at us!" the General cried, crashing the tank toward them.

The thieves squealed in terror. There was water blasting all around them, and they could see the hazy outline of the toy tank, grinding closer and closer.

The General whooped with glee. "Fire! Fire!" he cried, hitting the red button.

The jet of water shot out faster and faster from the toy gun, washing Mr. Goldtail and his mice across the floor.

"Stop!" the Chief Constable cried. "Stop firing and let me arrest them!"

But the thieves were being swept closer and closer to the

garden door, until eventually the water sprayed them onto the doormat. They finally managed to scramble upright, clinging to the rough matting.

"Run!" Mr. Goldtail cried. "Run for your lives!" And with the water blasting at their heels, all four mice fled under the door in terror.

"Stop them!" the Chief Constable cried.

He darted for the hatch and pushed it open. "Come on, let's get them!" he shouted.

He was about to fling himself outside, but then suddenly there was a bright glare. The kitchen lights had come on. The Chief Constable ducked back inside. And when the mice peered out through the sherbet-smudged windshield, they got the most terrible fright.

Arthur and Lucy had appeared!

# Chapter Fifteen

Arthur stared at the toy tank in astonishment.

"How did that get here?" he said. "I left it in the living room!"

Tumtum and the others looked at each other in horror. If Arthur opened the hatch of the tank, he was sure to find them.

But then suddenly the children heard a strange noise, like an engine revving, and the next moment they saw a light flicker under the garden door.

They ran and opened it, and when they saw outside they both gasped. For there was the toy bus, fleeing down the garden path!

"Catch it!" Arthur cried, stumbling onto the doorstep.

Lucy grabbed the flashlight from the shelf and ran after

him. And as the children rushed into the garden, Tumtum and the others slithered out of the tank and crept under the dresser.

They could hear the toy bus rattling down the path and the children chasing after it.

"Stop!" Arthur shouted — but the bus was going at full speed. Mr. Goldtail was driving it as fast as it would go, speeding toward a gap in the hedge.

"Faster! Faster!" the clowns all shrieked, looking through the back windshield in terror. But the children were catching up with them. And just as the bus was swerving onto the lawn, a huge pink hand appeared in the headlights and clamped over the windshield.

And when the mice looked in the side-view mirror, they saw Arthur unhitching the wagons from behind them. Then the bus was lifted high into the air.

They pushed on the doors, desperately trying to get out. But Arthur had shut the catches on the outside. They were locked in.

"Put us down!" cried Mr. Moody.

"*Let us go!*" roared Mr. Goldtail, thumping the window with rage.

The children shone their flashlight into the bus in amazement.

"It must be Mr. Goldtail and his gang!" Lucy said. "And look, they're even wearing circus clothes!"

Arthur and Lucy had met some very strange mice before. Even so, they were rather astonished.

"Aren't they extraordinary!" Lucy said. "I say, do you think it was *them* who broke into the village shop? Nutmeg said they were very wicked—so breaking into a village shop is just the sort of thing they might do!"

"Let's look in the wagons," Arthur said. "If they did raid the shop, then we'll probably find some of the things they stole."

They carefully carried the bus and the wagons back into the kitchen and set them down on the table.

Tumtum and the others watched excitedly from under the dresser. Then Nutmeg and Mrs. Marchmouse heard the commotion and came running out, too.

"Oh, thank goodness, you're all right," Nutmeg cried, clutching Tumtum's paw. "But you're soaked! Whatever's been going on?"

"Shh!" Tumtum said, pointing into the kitchen. "The children have caught Goldtail and his gang! They all tried to drive off in the toy bus, but Arthur and Lucy chased after them, and now they've locked them in!"

"Oh, how clever of them!" Nutmeg said proudly.

They all crouched very still, watching as the children searched the wagons.

When they opened the door of the first wagon, a beetle bounced out.

"Ugh!" said Lucy, stepping back in fright. The beetle scuttled about the table, then hopped to the floor and disappeared under the sink.

The next wagon was full of tiny cardboard boxes, sealed with brown tape. Arthur took out his pocketknife and carefully slit them open. When the children saw what they contained, they both gasped.

For each box was full of the tiniest, most exquisite

treasures! Gold plates and jugs, and candlesticks, and paintings and tapestries—all mouse-sized.

"These must be all the things they stole," Lucy said, spreading everything out on the table. "We shall have to give them to Nutmeg. I'm sure she can find out which mice they belong to and give them all back!"

The next three wagons were furnished with camp beds and dressing tables, and wardrobes containing tiny suits of clothes. And the last wagon was full of tubes of sherbet!

"Look!" Arthur said. "This must be the sherbet that was stolen from the village shop!" He reached into the wagon and pulled out one of the tubes. It had scuffs at the end, where it had been nibbled.

"Goodness," he said. "Just think how astonished Mrs. Paterson will be when she learns that the robbers were mice!"

Mr. Goldtail and the clowns could not bear to see their loot being touched. They beat the windows so hard that the bus started to shake.

"They're going to get out!" Arthur said anxiously. "Quick, let's get Pa. He'll know what to do with them!"

390

Lucy ran upstairs. Mr. Mildew was in his study, struggling with his latest invention — a mechanical pencil that could write and spell all by itself. He hardly looked up when Lucy came in. "What is it?" he muttered. "Didn't I say you were meant to stay in your room?"

"Oh, yes, but please come downstairs — we've got something to show you," Lucy said. "Oh, please come and see! Then you'll understand everything!"

Mr. Mildew grudgingly followed her downstairs. But when he saw what was on the kitchen table, his eyes bulged in astonishment.

"They're the ones who robbed the shop," Lucy said. "Look! Here's all the sherbet they took!"

Mr. Mildew hardly knew what to say. "I had better call Mrs. Paterson," he muttered. He picked up the telephone and in a trembling voice told her to come at once.

She hurried to Rose Cottage, wondering what could have happened. And when she saw the mice scrambling about in the toy bus, and the stolen sherbet, she was too astonished to speak.

It took two strong cups of tea to stop her shaking.

"What are we going to do with them?" Mr. Mildew asked, fearing the children might want to keep them as pets.

"Oh, we don't want them at Rose Cottage," Lucy said. "They're too noisy!"

"Perhaps we could find a cage for them, and keep them in the garden shed, where we wouldn't have to look at them all the time," Arthur said.

"*A garden shed!* How dare you!" Mr. Goldtail shouted, not liking the sound of this one bit.

"Oh, stop squealing!" Arthur said, rapping the bus with a spoon.

"They would be a waste in a shed!" Mrs. Paterson said, gathering her wits again. "They are MUCH too good for that. If you don't want them, I shall sell them for you at the village shop! I'll put an advertisement in the local newspaper, and sell them to whoever offers the most money! I'm sure they'll fetch a *fortune*. Four mice dressed in funny clothes, breaking into my shop, and driving off in a toy bus....They must be the cleverest mice in the whole wide world! Why, I wouldn't be surprised if they don't become stars on television!"

"Oh, what a good idea!" Lucy cried.

"And I shall give all the money to you," Mrs. Paterson said kindly. "And you can keep the sherbet, too! It's the least you deserve. I am sorry about this morning, my dears. It was quite wrong of me to accuse you of stealing."

"Oh, don't worry about that," Lucy said. This morning seemed like ages ago — the children were just glad things had turned out so well.

"I'll take them with me now," Mrs. Paterson said, tucking the bus firmly under her arm. "I've a nice big cage back at home I can put them in — it's one my niece used to use for her gerbils. Then I'll give your bus a good cleaning and bring it back to you in the morning, along with that poor old toy policeman, of course!"

Everyone laughed — and they didn't notice that the prisoners had become quiet. "The television, just think of that!" Mr. Moody whispered. "We'll be famous!"

"And rich!" Mr. Mirth tittered.

"Sounds better than driving round in a flea-bitten old circus!" Mr. Merry said.

In his mind's eye, Mr. Goldtail suddenly had a delicious image of himself dressed in dark glasses, being chauffeured between television studios in the back of a sleek limousine — and he decided things hadn't turned out so badly after all.

Tumtum and the others all cheered when Mrs. Paterson carried the thieves away.

"I shall telephone the *Mouse Times* first thing in the morning and tell them the burglars have been caught, and that it was all thanks to me — er, us!" the General said boastfully.

"And tomorrow I shall go around to all the local mouse holes, returning the stolen goods to their rightful owners," the Chief Constable said happily. "Just think how pleased they shall all be!"

They hid under the dresser, waiting until Mr. Mildew and the children had gone upstairs. "I shall go up to the attic tonight and write the children a letter, congratulating them on every-

thing they've done," Nutmeg said. "And I shall tell them to keep the wagons. They belong to Arthur's circus now!"

Everyone agreed. "And now let's have a celebration!" Tumtum said, leading them all back to Nutmouse Hall. "Have we anything to eat, dear?" he asked Nutmeg anxiously. "I feel quite hungry!"

"Why, of course!" Nutmeg replied. "We've got the General's birthday feast! The table's still set in the dining room, and the cake hasn't been touched!"

They all cheered. After such a grand adventure, a feast was just what they needed. Tumtum set two extra places for Mrs. Marchmouse and the Chief Constable, and soon they were all sitting down at the big oak table, feasting long into the night.

The birthday party was two days late, but all the better for it. The candles flickered and the cider flowed, and by the time Nutmeg carried in the cake, everyone had quite forgotten how badly the General had behaved.

They all sang "Happy Birthday" while tapping their silver teaspoons on the table.

The General glowed. What a wonderful adventure it had

turned out to be! And just think what a hero he would be when he told the *Mouse Times* how he had chased Mr. Goldtail from Nutmouse Hall in a toy tank!

"*For I'm a jolly good fellow!*" he sang, blowing out his candles with a single puff. And the mood was so merry, even the Chief Constable agreed that a better general there never was!

Arthur and Lucy climbed into bed in the attic, unaware of the festivities going on downstairs. They had left Nutmeg a letter on the chest of drawers, telling her everything that had happened — for they could not have guessed that she had been watching from beneath the dresser.

"Arthur," Lucy said hesitantly, "I was just thinking, and I know it's strange but . . . well, we've had so many funny adventures with mice, you don't think *Nutmeg* might be a mouse, do you?"

Nutmeg had told them in a letter that she was a Fairy of Sorts, and the children had always accepted this. But now Lucy was starting to have doubts.

"I suppose it's possible," Arthur said sleepily. "Well, she's

396

sure to come up here tonight and fetch the letter. Let's take turns to stay awake and watch the chest of drawers!"

"All right," Lucy said. "I'll keep watch first, then I'll wake you up at midnight, and you can take over."

Arthur muttered his agreement and quickly fell asleep. Lucy propped herself up on her pillow, watching the moonlight slip through the curtains. It was very exciting to think she might finally find out who Nutmeg was. But an hour passed, and then another, and her eyes got heavier and heavier. . . . And by the time Nutmeg finally crept upstairs, Lucy was far away, dreaming of mice dressed as clowns, and of fairies with long, nutmeg tails.

**Tumtum & Nutmeg's**

# Christmas Recipe Book

## Nutmeg's Cooking Tips

*Before you start, here are some tips to make sure your cooking is safe and enjoyable:*

- *Always ask an adult's permission before starting, and make sure you have an adult with you to help.*
- *Wash your paws with soap and water before you start.*
- *Always use oven mitts for moving things in or out of the oven, and remember, once you've taken something from the oven it will take a while to cool down.*
- *Remember to turn the oven off when you've finished cooking.*
- *Make sure you wash up after yourself!*
- *When you see an instruction marked \*, it means "Careful! Please ask an adult for help."*

# Mini Lemon Pancakes
### *(Makes roughly 15 pancakes)*

## Ingredients:

- 1 egg • 1 ⅔ cups of milk • 1 ½ cups of sifted all-purpose flour
- 3 ½ teaspoons of baking powder • 1 tablespoon of sugar
- 3 tablespoons of butter • Juice from a quarter of a lemon
- 2 tablespoons of confectioners' sugar

## Cooking Instructions:

1. Place the egg and the milk in a large mixing bowl and beat with a whisk until they form a bubbly mixture.
2. Sift in the flour, baking powder, and sugar, and whisk to form a smooth batter.
3. *Put the butter in a frying pan, and place on the stove on a medium heat. When the butter has melted, add a spoonful of the batter to the pan.
4. Allow the pancake to spread, and wait a couple of minutes until the edges turn golden.
5. Shake the pan to loosen the pancake from the bottom, and then use a spatula to flip it over.
6. Cook another couple of minutes, then turn the pancake out onto a plate.
7. Repeat these steps until all of the pancake mixture is used up, and then serve with lemon juice and a sprinkling of confectioners' sugar.

# Bubble and Squeak
### Serves 3

## Ingredients:

- ½ a cabbage • 1 small onion • 1 cup of leftover chopped vegetables (broccoli, carrots, peas, corn, anything)
- 1 cup of leftover mashed potatoes • 2 tablespoons of butter
- 2 tablespoons of olive oil

## Cooking Instructions:

1. *Cut the onion into small pieces and the cabbage into shreds.
2. Heat half of the oil in a small frying pan, then add the cabbage and onion and cook on a medium heat until soft.
3. Mix all the cooked cabbage, leftover vegetables, and mashed potatoes in a bowl, and season with salt and pepper.
4. Add the rest of the olive oil and butter to the pan, and then the vegetable mixture. Pat the mixture down with a spatula to form a large pancake.
5. Cook for about 10 minutes until the underside is golden brown but not burned, then turn over using the spatula.
6. Cook for another 10 minutes until both sides are the same golden brown color.
7. Remove to a plate and cut into slices.

**Nutmeg's Tips:** The frying pan needs to be small or the bubble and squeak will fall apart when you turn it over. This is also delicious cooked with bacon or ham.

# Strawberry Creams
### *(Makes 24 strawberry creams)*

## Ingredients:

- ½ cup of confectioners' sugar
- 1 cup of freeze-dried strawberries

*(available from most large supermarkets)*

- 3 tablespoons of condensed milk
- A few teaspoons of cool water
- Spare confectioners' sugar for dusting

## Cooking Instructions:

1. Line a baking tray or large plate with a piece of waxed paper.
2. Put the strawberries in a sealed plastic bag and crush them with a rolling pin until they form a fine red powder, then stir the powder and the confectioners' sugar together in a mixing bowl.
3. Add the condensed milk and mix to form a very firm dough. (If your dough is too dry to come together, add a teaspoon of cool water and continue mixing.)
4. When the dough is ready, dust a board with confectioners' sugar and lay the dough on it. Divide into 2 pieces, and roll each piece into a sausage about 6 inches long.
5. *Cut each sausage into 12 evenly sized pieces, dusting the knife with confectioners' sugar so the dough doesn't stick to it. Roll each slice into a ball and squash the end slightly so that it looks like a strawberry.
6. Place all of the pieces on top of the waxed paper or baking parchment and leave them there to dry for several hours.

**Nutmeg's Tip:** *Freeze-dried strawberries are eaten by astronauts on space flights, and they are the best thing to use for this recipe.*

### Picnic Pork Pie
#### Serves 4

## Ingredients:

- 1 sheet of frozen or chilled puff pastry
- 16 cooked cocktail sausages
- 1 tablespoon of onion chutney or ketchup
- 1 egg, beaten • Sprinkle of all-purpose flour

## Cooking Instructions:

1. *Preheat the oven to 400° F.
2. Thaw the sheet of puff pastry for 30 minutes and then lay it out on a cutting board dusted with flour.
3. Roll the pastry out flat on the board with a rolling pin and cut 4 squares about 5 inches long and 5 inches wide.
4. Spread the onion chutney or ketchup evenly over each square, leaving a ¼ inch gap all around the edge.
5. Stick four cocktail sausages in the middle of each square, and then fold the edges of the square around the sausages and squish the sides together to seal the pie.
6. Brush the beaten egg over the pastry and place on a greased baking sheet. Bake for 20 minutes until golden brown.

# Jellied Fruits
### Serves 4

## Ingredients:
- 1 package of raspberry gelatin
- 1 small basket of blueberries
- 1 small basket of blackberries
- 1 cup of boiling water • ¼ cup of cold water

## Cooking Instructions:

1. *Put the gelatin and the boiling water in a heat-proof glass bowl, and stir until all the crystals have disappeared.
2. Let the mixture cool for 30 minutes.
3. Pour the berries into the mixture, then stir in the cold water.
4. Cover the bowl and then return to the refrigerator to set for 24 hours.
5. Serve with cream and mint leaves.

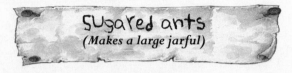

# Sugared ants
### (Makes a large jarful)

## Ingredients:

- 4 ounces of raisins
- ¼ cup of sugar
- ¼ cup of ground almonds
- ⅓ cup of melted butter

## Cooking Instructions:

1. Stir the sugar and the ground almonds together in a bowl.
2. *Melt the butter in a pan, and then pour the contents into a separate bowl and stir in the raisins.
3. Use a skimming ladle to transfer the buttery raisins to the sugar and almond mixture, and roll them around until they are fully coated.
4. Spread the sugared ants out spoonful by spoonful on a baking tray lined with foil. Leave them to crystallize overnight, then store in a large jam jar.

## Fireside Flapjacks
### Makes 12

### Ingredients:
- 4 cups of rolled oats
- ¼ cup of sugar
- ⅔ cup of butter
- 4 tablespoons of corn syrup

### Cooking Instructions:

1. *Preheat the oven to 375° F and grease a shallow, square baking pan with butter.
2. *Melt the butter, sugar, and syrup in a saucepan on a low heat, then remove from the heat and stir in the oats with a wooden spoon.
3. Pour the mixture into the pan and pat down gently to make sure it is even.
4. Put the pan in the oven for about 20 minutes, until the corners are brown but the middle is soft.
5. Leave to cool for 30 minutes, then cut into squares.